I've been in Little League for six years now. But to tell you the truth, I'm not what you'd call a real good athlete. Actually, I'm not even real fair. I'm more what you'd call real stinky.

Every year Alex Frankovitch—otherwise known as Skinnybones—receives the trophy for the Most Improved Player on his baseball team. That doesn't fool Alex, though. He knows that the only players who get that trophy are the ones "who stink to begin with." And with top-notch players like T.J. Stoner around to tease him, this season could end up being Alex's worst one yet.

Life looks hopeless when T.J. challenges Alex to a pitching contest (some contest!), and when Alex's new uniform (size small) is way too big, and especially when his losing team has to play T.J.'s winning one and a TV news crew decides to film that game! But Alex does have a hidden talent that could save the day, unless it ruins his whole life first. . . .

You'll laugh right along with Skinnybones in Barbara Park's new novel. It's the saddest, funniest baseball story of the season.

To Anderson Elementary!
Barbara Park
1986

Skinnybones

by BARBARA PARK

ALFRED A. KNOPF • NEW YORK

To Steven and David
for all your inspiration

THIS IS A BORZOI BOOK
PUBLISHED BY ALFRED A. KNOPF, INC.

Library of Congress Cataloging in Publication Data
Park, Barbara.   Skinnybones.
Summary: Alex's active sense of humor helps him get
along with the school braggart, make the most of his
athletic talents, and simply get by in a hectic world.
I. Title   PZ7.P2197Sk   1982   [Fic]   81-20791
ISBN 0-394-84988-4   AACR2
ISBN 0-394-94988-9 (lib. bdg.)
Manufactured in the United States of America
10 9 8 7 6

SKINNYBONES

chapter one

MY CAT EATS KITTY FRITTERS BECAUSE...

I figure that if she *didn't* eat Kitty Fritters, she would probably be dead by now.

Kitty Fritters is the only cat food my mother will buy. She buys it because she says it's cheap. She says she doesn't care how it tastes, or what it's made out of. My mother is not the kind of person who believes that an animal is a member of the family. She is one of those people who thinks a cat is just a cat.

I have an aunt who thinks that her cat is a real person. Every time we go over there, she has her cat dressed up in this little sweater that says FOXY KITTY on the front.

This aunt of mine wouldn't be caught dead giving her cat Kitty Fritters. She says that Kitty Fritters taste like rubber. I'd hate to think that my aunt has actually tasted Kitty Fritters herself, but how else would she know? My mother says that my aunt is a very sick person.

Anyway, I think you should keep on making Kitty Fritters as long as there are people like my mother, who don't think cats mind eating rubber.

THE END

After I finished writing, I went to the closet and took the bag of Kitty Fritters off the bottom shelf. I turned to the back of the bag and read the rest of the directions. It said:

COMPLETE THIS SENTENCE:
MY CAT EATS KITTY FRITTERS BECAUSE . . .
Then print your name and address on the entry
blank enclosed in this bag. Mail your entry to:

KITTY FRITTERS TV CONTEST
P. O. Box 2343
Philadelphia, Pennsylvania 19103

I dug down into the bag, trying to find the entry blank. I couldn't feel it anywhere. I tried again, reaching down into the other side of the bag. It wasn't there either. Finally I put the bag between my legs, and stuck both of my arms all the way down to the very bottom. I still couldn't find it!

Finally I got so frustrated, I dumped the entire ten-pound bag of cat food out onto the kitchen floor. I must have sifted through about a million little fritters before I finally found the entry blank. Carefully, I placed it on the kitchen counter and filled it out.

NAME: Alex Frankovitch
ADDRESS: 2567 Delaney Street
CITY: Phoenix   STATE: Arizona   ZIP: 85004

Just as I was finishing up, I heard the cat scratching at the door. I figured that she had probably smelled the disgusting odor of fritters all the way down the block.

"Go away!" I shouted. "You can't come in right now. I'm busy!"

I just *had* to get the cat food mess cleaned up before my mother got home.

"Alex Frankovitch! You open this door!" shouted my cat. My cat? Oh no! Suddenly, I realized that it had been my *mother* scratching at the door.

I hurried to let her in.

"Why were you scratching at the door?" I asked when I opened it. It was a very stupid question. She was carrying two large bags of groceries.

"I wasn't scratching," she answered as she hustled by me. "I banged on it with my foot!"

After putting the groceries on the counter, my mother glanced down at the millions of little fritters scattered all over the floor. All things considered, I think she took it very well.

"Been fixing yourself a little snack, Alex?" she asked, sounding slightly annoyed.

I figured that there were two different ways of handling my problem. First of all, I could try to get my mother to laugh about the whole thing. If *that* failed, I would have to move on to Plan Two: Blame It on the Cat.

"Snack? What snack?" I asked, trying to sound very serious. "I haven't been fixing a snack."

"I *mean* all these Kitty Fritters, Alex," said my mother, even more annoyed than before.

"Kitty Fritters?" I asked, looking all around. "What Kitty Fritters?"

This was where she was supposed to start laughing. But unfortunately, she didn't.

"I'm waiting for an explanation, Alex," she said, folding her arms. Whenever my mother folds her arms, she means business. Quickly, I moved on to Plan Two.

"Oh . . . *those* Kitty Fritters!" I said, pointing at the floor. "Well, you're probably not going to believe this, but while you were gone I was sitting in the den watching TV—"

"Now, *that* I believe," interrupted my mother. "It seems that all you've been doing lately is watching that stupid TV."

"Listen, Mother," I said, "do you want to hear what happened, or not?"

"Okay, Alex," she said, "you may continue."

"Well, anyway," I said, "there I was watching TV, when all of a sudden, I heard this loud crash come from the kitchen. I ran in here just in time to see the cat running out the back door. That's when I looked down and saw this giant mess of fritters."

My mother just stared at me for a minute. Then she said, "Are you *positive* that's what happened, Alex?"

I couldn't believe it. My mother was actually going to believe that stupid story. Wow! For the very first time, I was really going to get away with something. Usually I *never* get away with *anything*!

"Positive, Mom," I replied. "Honest, that's exactly what happened. The cat must have tried to get something to eat and knocked the bag over."

My mother walked over and put her hand on my shoulder. "In that case, Alex," she said, "could you please do me a big favor?"

"Aw, come on, Mom!" I said, trying to sound upset. "You're not going to make me clean this whole mess up, are you? That's really not fair. I just told you I didn't do it!"

"No, Alex, that's *not* what I wanted," she said with a very strange grin on her face. "What I want you to do is to go and get the cat out of the car. I just brought her home from the vet's. I took her to get her shots."

Now, most people think that when you get caught in a giant lie like that you're doomed. But not me. I've always said, "A good liar never gives up without a fight."

"Boy, that really makes me mad!" I shouted.

"What makes you mad, Alex?" asked my mother. "Being caught in a stupid, ridiculous lie like that?"

"Lie? What lie? What are you talking about, Mom? No," I said, "the thing that makes me mad is that one of Fluffy's little friends would come in here, make a big mess, and then try to run away and blame it on poor little Fluffy! Boy, when I find out which neighborhood cat did this, he's *really* going to be sorry."

Then I hurried outside and got Fluffy from the car. As I walked back into the house, I kept talking to the cat so that my mother wouldn't have a chance to say anything.

"Fluffy, you're not going to believe this, but one of your little buddies almost got you in very big trouble! If you ask me, I think it was probably Fritzi, from down the street. I've always thought that Fritzi was the sneaky type—"

"Alex . . . Alex!" shouted my mother, interrupting me.

"Yes, Mom?"

"Give up," she said.

"Give up?" I asked. "What do you mean, give up?"

"I mean, you're making a fool out of yourself, Alex," she said.

I paused for a minute and looked up. "Does this mean that you don't believe me?"

"Let me put it this way, Alex," my mother replied. "If you were Pinocchio, right now we'd have enough firewood to last the winter."

Then she handed me a broom and started out of the room.

"Don't look so glum," she said as she left. "If it

will make you feel any better, that was the most creative fib you've told in weeks."

I thought about it.

It didn't make me feel better.

As soon as she was gone, I started sweeping the Kitty Fritters back into the bag. Meanwhile, Fluffy had begun to eat every single fritter in sight.

I just couldn't seem to get the darned things back into the bag fast enough. Fluffy was really packing them in. Getting shots must give cats quite an appetite.

It took about ten minutes before I was finished cleaning up the floor. By that time, I could tell that Fluffy was getting pretty full. But she never stopped eating . . . not until the last Kitty Fritter was in the bag.

As I put the bag back on the bottom shelf, my mother came in to inspect the floor. The cat ran to greet her. My mother stared at her for a minute.

"Why does Fluffy look so puffy?" she asked.

"I guess it must be all those Kitty Fritters she ate while I was trying to get them cleaned up," I explained.

"Oh, Alex!" my mother cried. "Those things will swell up in her stomach and make her very sick! She's not supposed to have too many!"

10

My mother looked worried.

I would have been worried too, but just then Fluffy walked over to where I was standing and threw up on my shoe. It was the most disgusting thing that ever happened to me.

My mother started laughing.

"This is not funny!" I shouted. But my mother couldn't seem to stop. If you ask me, I think she was acting pretty childish.

After a couple of minutes, she walked over and picked up the cat. "Honestly, Fluffy," she said, "if you don't like Alex's shoes, all you have to do is *say* so." Then she started laughing all over again.

I think I probably would have felt a lot worse, but my mother was laughing so hard that she forgot to punish me for lying to her. Getting her to laugh always works. I just wish I could have done it without having Fluffy throw up on me.

chapter two

The first time that I can remember making people laugh was in kindergarten. Every morning, the teacher would ask if anyone had anything special for Show and Tell.

At first I was pretty shy. I would just sit there quietly at my desk and keep my mouth shut. But there were lots of kids who didn't.

There was this one kid named Peter Donnelly who sat in front of me. Every single day, when the teacher asked if anyone had anything for Show and Tell, dumb old Peter Donnelly would raise his hand.

Sometimes he brought in hobbies. Peter had the stupidest hobbies in the whole world. One of his hobbies was collecting different-colored fuzz. Weird, right?

One day he brought his fuzz collection to school. He kept it in a shoe box. When he passed it around, I felt stupid just looking at it.

Then, all of a sudden, I got this funny idea. Just as I was about to pass the box to the next person, I pretended that I was going to sneeze.

"AH . . . AH . . . AHCHOO!"

I sneezed right smack in the middle of Peter's fuzz collection. Fuzz balls went flying everywhere. The whole class began to laugh at once.

Peter panicked. He rushed over to my desk and began gathering up his fuzz collection and putting it back in his box. The teacher told me to help him, but I was laughing too hard to get out of my chair. I had to admit, making people laugh was a lot more fun than sitting quietly in my seat. I decided I would have to do it more often.

From then on, I began to use Show and Tell to tell the class funny things that had happened to me. When I ran out of true things to tell, I started making them up.

One time I told the class that my father was a raisin. I don't know what made me say such a silly thing. But it sure sounded funny.

The teacher made me sit down. She said that

there was a big difference between Show and Tell and Show and Fib. Personally, I don't think teachers like it when their students are funnier than they are. I ought to know. So far I've been funnier than every teacher I've ever had. And not one of them has liked me. My goal in life is to try and find a teacher who appreciates my sense of humor.

Last year I had a teacher named Miss Henderson. So far, out of all the teachers I've ever had, Miss Henderson is the one who disliked me the most.

I'm not really sure why. In the fifth grade, I was the funniest I've ever been. You'd think a teacher would like it when a student tries to brighten up the day with a little joke or two.

On the very first day of school, I knew Miss Henderson wasn't going to like me. She made everyone stand up next to their desk and introduce themselves to the class. Boy, do I hate that! You were supposed to tell your name, where you were born, and something about your family. Allison Martin started.

She said, "My name is Allison Martin. I was born right here in Phoenix, and I have two brothers."

Whoopee for you, I thought to myself.

Then, Brenda Ferguson stood up. "My name

14

is Brenda Ferguson. I was born in California, and I have a baby sister."

And you're also very dumb, I thought.

This had to be the most boring thing I had ever listened to in my life. After about six kids had spoken, I just couldn't stand it anymore. I raised my hand.

"Yes," said Miss Henderson. "You there, in the yellow shirt."

I looked down at my shirt. Yup. It was yellow all right. I stood up.

"Miss Henderson," I said, "this is getting kind of boring. Couldn't we try to tell something a little more interesting about ourselves?"

Miss Henderson thought about it for a minute and then gave me a little smile.

"Okay, then," she said finally. "Why don't you start us off? Tell us who you are and something interesting about yourself."

Wow! I thought to myself. Maybe for once, I've got a teacher who is going to appreciate me.

"Okay," I said. "My name is Alex Frankovitch. I was born in Phoenix, and my mother is a land turtle."

Miss Henderson didn't laugh. Instead she gave me a dirty look and motioned for me to sit down.

By this time, the whole class was roaring, and

15

Miss Henderson had to beat on her desk with a ruler. For a minute there, I actually started feeling a little sorry for her. But it didn't last long. As soon as she got the class under control, she continued with the same boring stuff we had been doing before.

After about an hour, we were almost finished. That's when I first noticed T. J. Stoner. He was sitting all the way in the back of the room. He was the very last person to tell about himself.

When he got up, he said, "My name is T. J. Stoner. I just moved here from San Diego. I have an older brother who plays baseball for the Chicago Cubs." Then he sat back down and tried to look cool.

Boy, do I hate it when kids try to look cool. I knew right away I wasn't going to like T. J. Stoner.

"That's very interesting, T.J.," said Miss Henderson. You could tell she was really impressed. "Could you tell us a little bit more about yourself?"

"Well, okay." T.J. stood up again. "My brother's name is Matt Stoner, and he plays third base. This is his second year in the majors."

"Do you play baseball, too, T.J.?" asked Miss Henderson.

"Yes," said T.J., "I'm a pitcher. Last year my team won the state championship in California. I was voted the Most Valuable Player."

"My goodness!" screeched Miss Henderson. "It really sounds as though you'll be playing for the Cubs someday yourself!"

Yuck! This whole conversation was making me sick! I raised my hand and began waving it all over the place. I could tell that Miss Henderson didn't want to call on me, but I was pretty hard to ignore.

"Yes?" she said, sounding disgusted.

I stood up. "Miss Henderson," I began, "I just thought that the class might like to know that I play baseball, too." She just kept staring at me, with her hands on her hips. I continued. "Last season, I played center field. At the end of the year, I was voted the Player with the Slowest Mother."

The whole class roared. Brenda Ferguson laughed so hard she almost fell off her chair. But two people didn't laugh at all. One was Miss Henderson. The other was T. J. Stoner.

I decided to sit down and keep my mouth shut for a while. The good thing about me is that I usually know when to quit. I may be funny, but I'm not stupid.

chapter three

Sometimes I think it would be fun to be a school principal . . . especially in the summer. A school principal spends his summers making up lists of all the kids in the school who hate each other. Then he makes sure he puts them together in the same class.

He really must have had a good laugh when he put T.J. and me in the same room again this year. Ever since I got sent to the principal for wearing wax lips to music class, he hasn't seemed to like me much.

When I first discovered the bad news about T.J., I hurried to tell my mother. I was hoping that maybe she could call the school and have me switched to a different classroom or something.

But no such luck. All my mother did was tell me that I should try to ignore him. She's always giving me great advice like that. Then she hands me my lunch, shoves me out the door, and her problems are over for the day. Mine are just beginning.

Last year, T. J. Stoner grew to be the biggest kid in the whole fifth grade. When I began to notice how big he was getting, I decided it might not be a bad idea to try to make friends with him. But unfortunately, T.J. didn't seem too interested. If I remember correctly, his exact words were, "Get lost, creep-head."

"Does that mean no?" I asked.

T.J. grabbed me by the shoulders and looked me straight in the eye. Then he said, "It means I hate your guts, Alex!"

"Aw come on, T.J.," I said, smiling. "Can't our guts be friends?"

T.J. didn't think that was quite as funny as I did. I could tell by the way he pushed me down and sat on my head. "Stop being such a jerk, you skinny bag of bones. You're beginning to get on my nerves." He gave me another shove and left. It's too bad my mother wasn't there. Maybe she could have told me how to ignore someone's knee when it's shoved in your mouth.

I think the worst thing about being in the same room with T.J. is having him in my gym class. I hate to admit it, but he's really a great athlete. For a kid, T. J. Stoner is the best baseball player that I've ever seen.

There's only one sport that I'm better at than T.J.—square dancing. I figure I can count square dancing as a sport because we do it in gym. You ought to see me. I can promenade my partner better than any other kid in the whole school.

One time I asked the gym teacher, Mr. McGuinsky, if he ever thought about starting a school square dancing team. I told him that if he did, I would like to volunteer to be the team captain.

He must have thought I was making a joke. He told me to sit my tail down and shut up. Gym teachers like to say "tail" a lot.

I do play other sports besides square dancing. Take Little League for instance. I've been in Little League for six years now. But to tell you the truth, I'm not what you'd call a real good athlete. Actually, I'm not even real fair. I'm more what you'd call real stinky.

I've got proof, too. Every single year that I've

played Little League, I've received the trophy for the Most Improved Player.

You may think that means I'm pretty good. That's what *I* used to think, too. But, over the past six years, I've noticed that none of the really good players ever gets the Most Improved Player award. And I finally figured out why. It's because the good players are already so good that they can't improve much. Let's face it, the only players on a team who can improve are the players who stink to begin with.

Last year, at the end of baseball season, I tried to explain how I felt to my father. We were sitting together at the Little League awards ceremony. The announcer began calling the names of all the players who were going to be receiving trophies.

I started to get very nervous.

"Just relax, Alex," said my father. "It won't be the end of the world if you don't win Most Improved again this year."

He just didn't understand at all.

"That's just it, Dad," I said, trying to explain. "I don't *want* to get Most Improved again. I don't mean to be a poor sport or anything, but if they call my name, why don't we just pretend we're not here. What do you say, Dad?"

I could tell by his face that my father was shocked. "Pretend we're not here!" he said loudly. "What kind of sportsmanship do you call that?"

"Shhh . . . Dad . . . not so loud," I said, trying to quiet him down. "It's just too embarrassing to get *another* Improved award, that's all. I just don't want it."

"I can't believe you!" my father exclaimed. "How ungrateful can you get, Alex? Do you know how many kids here would *love* to get that award tonight?"

"I know, Dad," I answered, "but that's only because most of them haven't figured out what the Most Improved trophy really means. They don't understand that getting that award means that you were *really* a stink-o player at the beginning of the season. Big deal. I'm supposed to be happy because I've gone from being stink-o to just smelly."

About that time, I heard my name being called over the microphone.

"Alex Frankovitch. Most Improved Player award for team number seven, Preston's Pest Control!"

When I heard it, I slid way down in my seat so that no one could see me. I could tell that my father was *very* annoyed with the way I was acting. He kept trying to grab my arm and make me stand up. Instead, I doubled over even further, and put my head between my knees.

The announcer called my name again. "Alex Frankovitch? Is Alex here?" he bellowed.

My father jumped up from his seat and pointed at me. At least that's what I *think* he did. I couldn't be sure. I was too busy trying to wad myself up into a little ball.

"Here he is, right here," screamed my dad. "Alex Frankovitch is right here!"

I guess everyone thought I was just being shy. The next thing I knew, the announcer shouted, "Let's give Alex a little applause to get him down here!"

Everyone started clapping. Then a few of the kids who knew me started shouting, "WE WANT ALEX . . . WE WANT ALEX!"

Finally, I had no choice. I stood up and started making my way down the bleachers. By the time I reached the fifth row, I had decided that I would never speak to my father again.

When I got to the bottom, I spotted T. J. Stoner. He was there getting another Most Valuable Player trophy. He kept pointing at me and laughing . . . pointing and laughing. . . .

I just couldn't let him get away with making fun of me. I decided that the only thing I could do was to pretend that I was really enjoying myself.

I walked to the middle of the gym floor, turned around, and started taking bows and throwing kisses. Then I walked over to the table to pick up my trophy.

The announcer handed me the microphone as I received my award. I was supposed to say thank you. But instead, I took the microphone, held it up to my mouth and burped.

The whole crowd started laughing at once. At least that's the way it sounded. Actually, I think the only people laughing were the kids. Usually, grownups don't think burping is quite as funny as kids do.

After that I decided to walk home. I knew I was in trouble, so I went straight to my room and waited for my father.

While I was waiting, I made a sign and hung it on the outside of my door. The sign said:

THIS ROOM BELONGS TO ALEX FRANKOVITCH,
THE ONLY BOY IN THE WHOLE WORLD
WHO HAS GONE FROM STINK-O TO SMELLY
SIX YEARS IN A ROW.

24

When my father saw the sign, he didn't even bother coming into my room to yell at me. I guess he figured I already felt bad enough.

He was right.

chapter four

For me, the worst part about belonging to Little League is the uniforms. Every year, the same thing happens. This year, at my second practice, it happened again.

The coach makes everyone line up to tell him what size shirt and pants they needed. He calls out a name and we shout out our size. We have three choices: small, medium, or large.

I checked out the other kids on my team. There were twelve of us all together. I figured that out of our whole team there were five larges, six mediums, and one teeny-tiny . . . me.

Every single year I am the smallest kid on the team. For a long time, I actually thought that I was a midget.

I remember when I was in first grade our teacher asked us to cut out magazine pictures of what we thought we would look like when we grew up. Most of the guys in my class brought in pictures of baseball or football players. A couple of others brought in pictures of policemen.

I brought in a picture of a Munchkin.

I got it out of *TV Guide*. Munchkins are the short little guys that keep running all over the place in the movie, *The Wizard of Oz*.

I think my teacher was surprised when she saw my picture. She called me up to her desk.

"Alex, what is this a picture of?" she asked.

"It's a Munchkin," I answered.

"That's what I was afraid of," she said.

"Oh, you don't have to be afraid of Munchkins, Mrs. Hurley," I said. "They're too short to hurt anyone."

"I *know* that they're short, Alex," she replied. "What I don't understand is why you want to be one when you grow up."

"I don't," I answered. "I want to be a baseball player."

"Then why did you bring in this picture?" asked Mrs. Hurley.

"Because *that's* what I'm going to look like," I explained. "You said to bring in a picture of what we were going to *look* like, didn't you?"

27

I guess Mrs. Hurley must have been worried about me. When I got home from school that day, she had already called my mother. As soon as I walked in the door, Mom sat me down and had a nice long talk with me about midgets.

"Alex," said my mother, "I know that you think you're too short. But that's only because you haven't started to grow as much as some of the other kids. Everyone grows at *different* speeds. But, believe me, you are going to grow! You are *not* going to be a Munchkin."

Then she took me by the hand and led me to the kitchen. She stood me up against the wall near the corner and told me not to move.

For a minute I thought she was going to try to shoot an apple off my head or something. Instead, she got a pencil and made a mark on the wall behind me. When I moved away, she wrote the date right next to it.

"Now," she said, "just to prove to you how much you're growing, we will measure you every six months. You won't believe it until you see it."

Well, all I can say is six months is a long time to wait . . . especially when you're waiting to find out whether or not you're a midget.

When the day finally came to measure me again, I was pretty nervous about it.

28

My mother stood me up against the wall in the same spot where I had been measured before. Then she carefully made another pencil mark. When I turned to look at it, I was *very* relieved. I had grown almost half an inch.

"Now do you believe me?" asked my mother. "Does this prove to you that you're not going to be a Munchkin?"

"Yeah, I guess so," I answered. "Now, if I could only figure out a way to put on some weight."

My mother threw her hands in the air. "I give up!" she shouted. "Honestly, Alex, if it's not one problem, it's another!" Then she just shook her head and left the room.

Sometimes my mother doesn't understand me at all. Being small is not an easy thing to be. Especially when you have to shout it out in front of your whole entire baseball team.

"Alex Frankovitch?" yelled my coach, "Small, medium, or large?"

I just couldn't bring myself to say 'small.' In fact, I guess you could say I panicked.

"Large!" I shouted.

Everyone on the team turned around to look at me. A couple of them laughed.

The coach walked over to me.

"Did you say 'large,' Alex?" he asked.

"Yes sir," I answered. "Large."

"Are you *sure* that large is the size you take, Alex?" he asked.

"Oh, no sir," I answered. "I usually don't take a large."

The coach looked relieved. "Well, what size do you usually take?"

"Extra large," I answered.

He just looked at me for a minute and then scribbled something down on his paper. As he walked away he mumbled something to himself that sounded a lot like "bubble-head." But I really didn't care what he thought. At least I didn't have to shout out 'small' in front of the whole team.

I figured that the day the uniforms came would be the best day of my entire life. I even had a dream about it.

In my dream, the coach had all the uniforms arranged in two piles . . . small and large.

Then he stood up and began calling out our names and sizes. When your name and size were called, you were supposed to go to the correct pile and select your uniform.

"Alex Frankovitch . . . large!" he shouted, loud enough for everyone to hear.

Slowly, I stood up and walked over to the large pile to choose my pants and shirt. When I got there, I realized that my uniform was the only one in the large pile. Everyone else on my team was a small. As I reached down to pick up my large shirt, everyone started to clap.

It was the best dream I ever had.

Finally, after waiting for three whole weeks for my dream to come true, the team uniforms came in. I was so excited I could hardly stand it.

When I got to practice that day, I noticed that the coach had arranged the uniforms in three piles. My heart started pounding wildly. It was almost like my dream. I felt like I had seen into the future or something.

Everyone lined up and the coach told us to go to the correct pile and pick out a uniform. This wasn't quite as good as if he had called out my name and size, but I really didn't mind. All I really cared about was having everyone see me at the large pile.

As soon as it was my turn, I rushed over and grabbed a large shirt and a pair of pants. I hung around the pile for a few seconds so everyone could see me, and then I took my uniform and stood back so the other kids could get theirs. When all the piles were gone, the coach told us to check our uniforms to make sure we had chosen the right size.

All of a sudden, I heard a few of the guys start to laugh. I turned around and saw Randy Tubbs trying to pull his new shirt over his head. It was stuck on his ears. Randy Tubbs is the biggest kid on our team. His head probably weighs as much as my entire body.

"Hey, Coach," he shouted, "I think I've got a little problem here!"

The coach walked over and helped Randy get the shirt off his head. Then he looked inside to see what size it was.

"This is a small, Randy," he said. "You ordered a large."

"Yeah," said Randy, "but this was the only uniform left when I got there."

The coach started looking all around. All of a sudden, I got this real sick feeling in my stomach. I tried to sneak off the practice field, but as I was walking away, he spotted me.

"Hold it, Alex," said the coach. "Bring your uniform over here for a minute, would you?"

As I handed the coach my shirt and pants, I checked the tag. "See, Coach? It's a large, just like you ordered for me," I said.

"Alex, I ordered you a small," he said. Then

he gave my uniform to Randy and handed me the small.

Boy, did that ever make me mad. What gave him the right to steal my uniform like that?

Randy held up his new shirt. "Now *that's* better!" he said, smiling.

When I got home I tried on my uniform. I sure didn't have any trouble getting it over my head. Good old Randy had really stretched the neck out of shape. It hung down to my stomach!

My mother told me not to worry about it. She said the shirt would probably shrink a little when it was washed. I didn't tell her, but I wished the pants would shrink too. They were way too big.

chapter five

T. J. Stoner brags about his baseball team more than any kid I've ever known in my whole life. So what if his team hasn't lost a game all year? It doesn't mean they won just because of T.J. Everyone knows that one kid can't make the difference between a winning team and a losing team. After all, every team *I've* ever been on has come in last place. And I don't care what anyone says, all those teams didn't lose just because of me.

This year I happen to know that I am not the worst player on my team. The worst player on my team is Ryan Brady. Ryan doesn't help us out at all. The very first game of the season, Ryan broke

34

his arm. Now all he does is sit on the bench. I'm sure I help the team out a lot more than Ryan.

I play center field. A lot of kids think that if you play in the outfield, it means you stink. My father says that's ridiculous. He says that outfielders are just as important as infielders. He told me that when he was a boy, he played in the outfield just like me. But that doesn't really make me feel much better. I've seen my father play baseball. He stinks.

My mother says that when people like T. J. Stoner brag, it's just because they're trying to get attention. And, as usual, she says to ignore them. But, for some reason, whenever I hear T.J. start to brag about his baseball team, I just can't seem to keep my mouth shut.

One day, a couple of weeks ago, I heard him talking to a bunch of kids out on the playground.

"My coach told me that for a kid, I was the best pitcher he had ever seen in his life," he said.

When I heard *that*, I did a very dumb thing. I called over to my friend Brian Dunlop. "Hey, Brian," I shouted, "I forgot to tell you. Last night, at baseball practice, my coach let me pitch. And boy, was he impressed! He said that I threw the fastest ball he had ever seen!"

I *know* it was a ridiculous thing to say, but

Brian sure wasn't much help. When he heard what I was saying, he fell on the ground and started laughing. I guess I really couldn't blame him, though. Brian has seen me throw.

Pretty soon, T.J. came strolling over. He bent over to talk to Brian. "Did I hear Skinnybones say that he can throw a fast ball?"

Brian couldn't stop laughing long enough to answer, so he just nodded his head.

T.J. stood up and walked over to where I was standing. "Hey, Frankovitch," he said, "I'll make you a little deal."

"Gee, I'm sorry, T.J.," I answered, shaking my head. "If you're going to try and get me to come pitch for your team, you're too late. The Yankees already called me this morning."

Brian let out another wild scream of laughter. T.J. joined him. I guess the idea of me pitching was even funnier than I thought.

One time I tried pitching with my dad. But it really didn't work out very well. Most of the balls I threw didn't even make it to the plate. Eight of them bounced in the dirt. The only ball that made it over the plate beaned him on the head.

"What kind of a stupid pitch was that?" shouted my father as he rubbed his head.

"I call it my old bean ball!" I shouted back.

I guess he wasn't in the mood for jokes that day. We packed up our stuff and went home.

Anyway, after T.J. finally stopped laughing about my big offer from the Yankees, he started bugging me again.

"Come on, Alex," he begged, "just listen to my deal. What have you got to lose?"

By this time a bunch of kids had started to gather around us. I think most of them had come over to see what was wrong with Brian.

"Okay, T.J.," I said, "tell me your deal. But make it snappy. It's almost time for Brian to massage my pitching arm."

"Okay," said T.J. "This is it. Since we're both such good pitchers, let's hold a contest after school to see who's the best. We'll even get a couple of kids to be the official umpires. What do you say, Frankovitch, is it a deal or not?"

Geez, what a mess I was in! If I said no, everyone would think I was chicken. But, if I said yes, everyone would be able to see how badly I pitched. I just had to get out of it!

I thought about it for a couple of minutes before I answered. "Gee, I'd really *love* to, T.J.," I answered finally. "But my coach told me not to tire my arm out by being in any stupid pitching contests. Thanks anyway."

37

I started to walk away but T.J. grabbed me by the shoulders. "You get one of your friends, Frankovitch, and I'll get one of mine. They'll be the umps. I'll meet you at the Little League field after school. If you're not there, we'll all know it's just because you're chicken."

As he turned to walk away, he stopped and looked back at me. "Be there, creep-head!" he shouted.

After he was gone, I looked down at Brian. He was still on the ground.

"Hey, Brian," I said, "how would you like to be an umpire this afternoon?"

Brian nodded his head. I think his sides were still hurting from all that laughing.

I reached my hand out to help him up. Together, we started back to class.

"Geez, Brian," I said, "if you think this is funny, wait until you see me pitch."

Then both of us started laughing. I figured I'd better laugh now while I had the chance.

chapter six

I was hoping the afternoon would drag on and on, but before I knew it the three o'clock bell rang. My teacher, Mrs. Grayson, dismissed the class.

I didn't want to go.

"Listen, Mrs. Grayson," I said, as she was getting ready to leave. "How would you like some help cleaning the boards and erasers this afternoon?"

"No thanks, Alex," she replied, "I've got a meeting to go to."

"Mrs. Grayson!" I said, trying to sound shocked, "I'm surprised at you! Do you mean to tell me that you are actually going to leave the room looking like a pig pen?"

"Please, Alex," she replied, "no jokes, okay? I'm really in a hurry." She held the door open for me to leave.

"Exactly what kind of meeting are you going to, Mrs. Grayson?" I asked.

"It's just a teachers' meeting, Alex, that's all. But I don't want to be late, so let's go, huh?"

"Listen, Mrs. Grayson," I continued. "How would you like it if I came along with you? That way, if the meeting got real boring, we could play tic-tac-toe, or something."

Mrs. Grayson stopped rushing me out the door. "Alex, is there some *reason* that you don't want to leave school today?" she asked. "Are you in some sort of trouble?"

"Trouble? Me?" I answered. "Oh no, Mrs. Grayson. Not me! I was just trying to make your meeting a little more fun, that's all."

"Well, thanks anyway, Alex," she said, "but I think I'll be able to stay awake today."

"Okay, have it your own way," I said, "but don't say I didn't try to help. I guess I'll just be heading on home now, Mrs. Grayson. That is, unless you'd like me to stick around until after your meeting's over to help you erase the boards. . . ."

I think Mrs. Grayson was getting a little

annoyed with me. "Go home, Alex!" she shouted.

So I did. I went home and got my ball and glove. Then I called Brian and told him to meet me at the Little League field.

By the time I got there, everyone else was already waiting for the contest to begin. And, when I say everyone, I mean *everyone*. There must have been about a million kids standing around waiting for me to make a big fool out of myself.

"Hey, Frankovitch!" shouted T.J., when he saw me coming. "For a minute there, I didn't think you were going to show up. What took you so long? Were you home plucking your feathers?"

I think this was his way of calling me a chicken again.

"A turkey like you probably knows a lot about feathers, T.J.!" I shouted back.

A few of the kids standing around started to laugh. T.J. wasn't one of them. He walked over to me.

"This is what we're going to do, Frankovitch," he began, seriously. "I brought along a catcher. He'll be catching for both of us."

I looked over at the kid in the catcher's mask. It was Hank Grover, one of T.J.'s best friends.

"Not fair! Not fair!" I protested. "I should have gotten to bring my own catcher, too!"

"What difference does it make who catches?" he asked. "The catcher isn't going to call balls or strikes. The umpires are going to do that. And besides, Alex," he added, "none of your jerky little friends knows how to catch."

Boy, did that ever make me mad! Insulting my friends like that! I probably should have punched him right in the mouth. Except for one tiny little problem. He was right. None of my jerky little friends *can* catch.

"Okay," T.J. continued, "we're each going to pitch ten balls. Your umpire and my umpire will stand together behind home plate. Then, as each ball is thrown, they will decide whether it's a strike or a ball. And to make it fair, the umpires *have* to agree on every call. If they can't agree, the pitcher takes the whole thing over again. Does that seem fair to you, Frankovitch?"

"Yeah, I guess so," I said. By this time I was getting nervous. All I *really* wanted to do was go home.

T.J. took a dime out of his pocket. "We'll flip to see who gets to pitch first," he said.

"Gee, I'm really sorry, T.J.," I said. "But I guess we won't be able to have this contest after all. I never learned how to flip. Maybe we could just somersault to see who goes first."

"Very funny. Now, heads or tails?" he yelled as he threw the coin in the air.

"Tummies," I hollered, trying to look very serious.

"Listen, Alex!" he yelled. "Knock off the funny stuff. Now . . . I'm going to toss this up one more time—heads or tails?" he shouted again.

I called tails.

It was heads. A bad sign.

"Okay," said T.J., "I won the toss, so I'll go first."

He took his ball and glove to the pitcher's mound. T.J.'s umpire, Eddie Fowler, and my umpire, Brian, took their places behind home plate. I hated to admit it, but having two umpires really did seem very fair. The trouble was, it seemed a little too fair. Before T.J. started pitching, I decided to have a little talk with Brian. I called him over.

"Listen, Brian," I said, "just because T. J. Stoner happens to be the very best pitcher that we've ever seen, doesn't mean that he's *perfect*. So, whatever you do, don't be afraid to call one of his pitches a ball if you really think it's a ball. And I don't want you to think that I would ever try to get you to cheat or anything, but keep in mind that I will be glad to pay you a dime for every ball you call—"

T.J. saw me talking to Brian and shouted, "Hey, Alex, don't bother trying to get Brian to cheat for you. I told him before you got here that if I caught him cheating, I'd break his face."

Brian looked at me and smiled. "Sorry, Alex," he said, "but I think I'd rather keep my face than make a couple of lousy dimes."

I was doomed.

T.J. was all set. "I'm ready!" he shouted.

"Ready?" I yelled back. "Aren't we even going to get a couple of practice pitches or anything?"

"You can practice if you *need* to, Frankovitch," he hollered, "but I don't really want any."

T.J. went into his windup. Some kids look dumb when they're winding up. But T.J. looked just like Steve Carlton.

Then he threw. The ball hit the catcher's mitt at about sixty miles an hour. But even worse, it hit his glove *exactly* in the center.

"Strike one!" shouted both umpires together.

T.J. didn't even blink an eye. He just got ready to throw the next pitch.

"Strike two!" shouted the umpires as the

second pitch crossed the middle of the plate.

This time, T.J. looked over in my direction and smiled. I leaned down and pretended I was tying my shoe so I wouldn't have to look at him.

"What's the matter, Alex?" he shouted. "Is the ball flying by so fast that it's untying your shoes?"

Then he laughed and got ready for his third pitch. As usual, it was perfect. The guy was really beginning to make me sick.

Every single pitch he threw came whizzing over the plate so fast you could hardly even see it. The catcher never even had to move a muscle. The ball hit the center of his mitt ten times straight! It was really disgusting.

"Okay, Skinnybones," he yelled after he'd thrown his last pitch, "it's your turn."

As T.J. sat down on the sidelines, Brian walked over and patted me on the back.

"Some friend you turned out to be, Brian," I said angrily. "What's the matter, did you forget how to say the word 'ball'?"

"Oh, get off it, Alex," he answered. "All his pitches were perfect. You really didn't expect me to cheat, did you?"

"Great, Brian," I said. "I'll remember how you feel about cheating the next time you need help on a math test."

Then I grabbed my glove and slowly walked out to the pitcher's mound. I was hoping that maybe, if I walked slowly enough, it would be dark by the time I got there and everyone would have to go home to dinner. But unfortunately, when I got to the mound the sun was still shining. There was no getting out of it now. I took a deep breath and turned around.

Oh no! It was a lot farther to home plate than I remembered. I began to panic. I can't throw all the way from here! I thought to myself. I'm so far away, the two umpires look like midgets!

Just then the two umpires stood up. Whew! That was a close one. They must have sat down when they saw how long it was taking me to get out to the mound.

The umpires lined up behind home plate and the catcher got set.

"Are you ready yet, Skinnybones?" yelled T.J. "Or do you want to practice first?"

Aha! A perfect opportunity to stall for time! Slowly, I walked off the mound and headed for T.J. on the sidelines. As soon as I got there he stood up. I stood on tiptoe and tried to look him in the eye.

"For your information, T.J.," I said, trying to act tough, "there is nothing skinny about my bones. So I would appreciate it if you would stop calling me that stupid name."

T.J. grabbed hold of my arm and held it up next to his.

"If your bones aren't skinny," he said, "then why is my arm so much bigger than yours?"

"You've got fat skin," I said simply.

T.J.'s eyes started getting real squinty. That meant he was about to hit me, so I hurried back out to the mound before he had a chance.

I stood there for a few minutes trying to figure out how to begin my windup. But pretty soon some of the kids started shouting at me to hurry up. So finally I was forced to begin.

I pulled my glove back toward my chest and stared at the catcher's mitt. Then I raised my left leg high in the air and hopped on my right foot.

Both of the umpires started to giggle. The catcher fell right over in the dirt laughing. They didn't even give me a chance to throw.

"Time out!" I yelled. "No fair! Interference on the umpires and the catcher!"

For once in his life, T.J. seemed to agree with me. He went over and tried to get the three of them to calm down. It took a few minutes, but finally they got themselves under control.

Once again, I went into my windup. I pulled

my glove back to my chest, raised my left leg high into the air, hopped on my right foot, and let the ball go.

I watched carefully as it rolled all the way to the plate. Wow! I thought to myself. What a pitch! It was a little low, of course, but at least I had it going in the right direction.

"Ball one!" shouted both umpires together.

"Well, I guess that's it, T.J.," I called as I walked off the mound. "I lost. One little mistake on my first pitch and it's all over. There's no way I can win, or even tie your pitching record when I've already got a ball. It's really a shame, too. That's probably the only bad pitch I'd have thrown all day."

"Not so fast, Frankovitch!" screamed T.J. running after me. He caught up to me and grabbed me by the collar. "You have nine more balls to throw, hot shot. We had a deal. So get back to that mound and we'll just see how good you are."

I knew there was no sense trying to argue with him. So slowly I turned around and headed back. Maybe there's still hope, I thought. If only I could throw a couple of good solid strikes, just one or two, at least I wouldn't end up looking like such an idiot.

I took a deep breath and got ready to throw my second pitch. My windup was the same, but something terrible happened when I started to throw. As I took the ball behind my head, it slipped out of my hand and landed in the dirt three feet behind me.

By this time I had really had it. All I wanted to do was get the whole thing over with quickly so I could go home and die. Brian had fallen in the dirt laughing. His mouth formed the words "Ball two," but nothing came out. I wound up and threw my third pitch as hard as I could.

T.J. was still watching from the sidelines. Unfortunately, my aim was a little bit off and the ball hit him in the arm.

"Strike one!" I shouted myself.

T.J. came running over holding his arm. "What do you mean, strike one?" he demanded, grabbing my shirt.

"Well, it struck you, didn't it?" I said, giggling.

"Let's see how you like being struck, Skinny-bones," he yelled, punching my arm as hard as he could.

Then he punched me again.

"Just remember what this feels like the next time you want to hit me with a ball," he growled. Somehow I got the feeling the contest was over.

My arm was a goner. It just hung limp at my side like it had croaked or something. I checked it out to see if it was bleeding, but no such luck. I hate that. When something hurts as bad as my arm did, the least it could do is bleed a little.

As T.J. walked away a lot of kids started running after him. Most of them were patting him on the arm and telling him what a great pitcher he was.

It's a good thing I didn't win. If anyone had patted me on my arm, I'm sure it would have fallen right off into the dirt.

I waited around a few minutes to walk home with Brian, but he must have left without me. At first I was mad about it, but in a way I understood. I guess he was just too embarrassed to walk home with a loser. I knew exactly how he felt. I didn't want to walk home with me, either.

chapter seven

Sometimes I wonder why I even bother to play baseball at all. I hate the uniforms, I can't throw, and I don't like playing center field. Lately I've been giving this a lot of thought, and there's only one thing I can come up with. . . .

I play for the caps.

Baseball caps are probably the greatest invention of all time. No matter what you look like, as soon as you put on a baseball cap you look just like Steve Garvey. Even my cat looks like Steve Garvey with my cap on.

Once I did an experiment with my grandmother just to prove it. My grandmother's about eighty years old, but she doesn't look it. She doesn't need a cane and she only wears glasses when she reads.

One of the things I like best about my grandmother is her blue hair. It's just about the coolest hair I've ever seen. I'm not sure that she really knows it's blue. I think she might be a little bit color-blind. One time at dinner she told my mother that she puts a "steel gray" rinse on it. I started to tell her that it looked more like "steel blue," but my mother stuck a roll in my mouth.

Anyway, after we finished eating that night, I ran up to my room and grabbed my baseball cap. Then I snuck up behind my grandmother and put it on her head. Just as I thought! Another Steve Garvey!

My grandmother wasn't a very good sport about it. She pulled my cap off her head and dropped it on the floor. Boy, I had really messed up her blue hair! In fact it was so messy that, right at the top of her head, I noticed a little bald spot. I offered to let her put my cap back on but she ignored me. I really felt sorry for her. She must have gone to the same barber I go to. My barber, Mr. Peoples, has given me more bald spots than I can even count.

I'll never forget the time he made my head look like a grapefruit. As soon as I walked in his shop that day, I knew I was in trouble. I always think it's a good idea to find out what kind of mood Mr. Peoples is in before I sit down in his chair. Sometimes when barbers aren't feeling very happy, they like to give kids funny haircuts to cheer themselves up.

"Hi, Mr. Peoples," I said with a smile. "How are you feeling today?"

Mr. Peoples looked at me and frowned. "I'll tell you how I'm feeling," he growled. "I'm hot, tired, and hungry. Any more questions?"

"Ah . . . no, Mr. Peoples, no more questions," I said as I began backing out of his shop. "Gee, I think I hear my mother calling. Maybe I'd better come back tomorrow."

"Knock it off, Alex, and sit down," he ordered, giving me a real disgusted look. Mr. Peoples has known me since I was two, so he thinks he can talk to me like that.

"Are you positive you want me to sit down?" I asked. "I mean, if you're not in a good mood I'd be happy to leave you alone for a little while."

"Sit!" he said gruffly, pointing to the chair.

Slowly I climbed into the big red seat. "Well, okay," I agreed. "But I really don't need a big haircut. I'd just like you to take a little bit off the sides. Okay?"

Mr. Peoples didn't hear a word I said. He was too busy plugging in his electric clippers.

"Wait a minute, Mr. Peoples!" I said quickly. "Do you really think you need the clippers today? I just want a little trim, remember?"

"Who's the barber here, Alex, you or me?" he asked sharply.

That's when I decided to be quiet. If there was one thing I didn't want to do, it was make the guy any madder than he already was.

Mr. Peoples started clipping. No wait . . . clipping is the wrong word. Mr. Peoples started scalping.

"You would have made a great Indian, Mr. Peoples," I said. But the clippers were so loud, he didn't hear me.

He whizzed those loud buzzing clippers all around the back of my head and headed up toward my ears.

All of a sudden, I heard him say, "Whoopsie!"

"Whoopsie?" I asked, nervously. "Did you just say 'whoopsie,' Mr. Peoples?"

I looked in the mirror. Right over my left ear, I saw the 'whoopsie.' It was a big round bald spot.

"This may be just a little bit shorter than you wanted it, Alex," said Mr. Peoples. "But at least it will be nice and cool for the summer."

54

"Nice and cool?" I asked angrily. "How do you figure that? If there are anymore 'whoopsies' I'll have to spend the whole summer wearing a big brown bag over my head. Have you ever spent the summer in a paper bag, Mr. Peoples?"

"Look on the bright side, Alex," he replied. "Think how easy it will be to take care of. Instead of combing through a lot of hair, all you'll have to do is polish your head a little." Then he laughed.

I couldn't stand to look in the mirror anymore so I closed my eyes and waited until he was finished. After circling my head with the clippers about twenty more times, he finally shut them off.

Slowly I opened my eyes and looked into the mirror. I couldn't believe it! I've seen more hair on an egg! I turned my head and looked at it from every angle hoping to find hair. But it was all gone.

"How do you like it?" asked Mr. Peoples, handing me a mirror.

"How do I like what?" I growled.

"Your hair, of course," he answered.

I gazed down at the floor. "I liked it a lot better when it was on my head," I replied as Mr. Peoples got the broom and started to sweep my hair into the dustpan.

He laughed. "I guess that means you think it's a little too short, huh?"

"No, Mr. Peoples," I answered. "If it was too short, at least some of it would still be growing out my head. I'd say it's too gone."

He laughed again. "That will be five dollars," he said, holding out his hand.

I slapped the money down and ran home as fast as I could. My mother met me at the door.

"Look what that butcher did to me!" I yelled, pointing to my head.

My mother stared at me for a minute. I could tell she was having a hard time trying not to laugh. "Don't worry," she said, finally getting control of herself. "The good thing about hair is that it always grows back."

"Yeah well, that might be the good thing about hair," I snapped, "but what's the good thing about no hair?"

My mother started to giggle. Then she turned and left the room.

"Where are you going?" I yelled. "You've got to help me figure out what to do with all this scalp!"

"I'll be right back," she answered, still snickering. "I'm just going to the kitchen for a minute.

All of a sudden I have this tremendous craving for grapefruit."

"Very funny!" I screamed at her. "Very, very, funny!"

Anyway, right after that I remembered about my baseball cap. I hurried up to my room to find it. I opened up my closet and breathed a sigh of relief. For once I had remembered to put it back on the hook where it belonged. I put it on my head and it slipped down a little bit. Being bald makes your head a lot thinner. I looked in the mirror. Yup. Just like old Steve Garvey! It works every time.

I just wish that putting on a baseball cap could make me hit home runs like Steve Garvey. I guess you could say that hitting a home run is sort of a dream of mine. I don't think it will ever come true, though. My father says that it's pretty hard to hit a home run when all you can do is bunt.

I've always thought "bunt" was a stupid word. The first time I heard it I was only about seven. This kid on my baseball team was on his way up to bat. Before he left the bench, he turned around and said to me, "I think I'm going to bunt."

At first I didn't really know what he was

talking about, but whatever it was, it didn't sound too good. I tried to figure out what he meant, and finally decided that "bunt" was probably another word for "puke."

Oh no, I thought to myself, that kid's sick and no one even knows it! I got off the bench and went running over to the coach and told him that I thought the kid was going to start bunting any minute.

"That's okay, Alex," said the coach, "don't worry about it. I *told* him to bunt."

Now, I was really confused. Why in the world would a coach tell one of his players to throw up? What kind of a trick was this? I hoped he wouldn't tell me to bunt, too.

"Listen, Coach," I said, "I don't think I could bunt even if I wanted to. I feel pretty good and I haven't even eaten dinner yet."

The coach looked at me kind of funny and told me to sit down. I went back to the bench and watched the kid at bat. I wondered when he was going to do it. When the ball came, he took his bat and held it out to the side. I figured he was just trying to get it out of the way so he didn't bunt on it. Since I was next at bat, I thought this was a pretty nice thing to do.

But, instead of getting sick, the kid took the

bat and lightly knocked the ball down the third baseline. He ran as fast as he could and made it to first base in plenty of time.

"Great bunt!" shouted the coach.

I turned to the boy sitting next to me. "I didn't see him bunt. Where is it?"

"Where is what?" he asked.

"You know," I said. "Where is the bunt?"

"Weren't you watching?" he asked. "He just bunted the ball down the third baseline and then ran to first."

Suddenly, I knew what a bunt really was. Brother, did I ever feel like an idiot! Thank goodness no one ever knew what I had been talking about.

Anyway, from that day on, I started working on my bunting. And after four years of practice, I'm probably the best bunter in the entire Little League. I guess that's because no one else bothers working on it very much.

Sometimes Brian helps me practice my bunting at recess. Last week, T.J. saw me and walked over.

"Bunting's for sissies," he said, grinning.

I ignored him.

"Anybody with half a muscle can hit the ball hard," he said.

I still ignored him.

"Hey, Skinnybones, I just thought of something," he said with a smile. "Only runts bunt! Get it? It rhymes!"

That's when I decided to stop ignoring him. Brian pitched me another ball. I held the bat out until the very last minute. Then I turned it sharply so that the ball hit T.J. right on the head.

"Whoops! Sorry there, T.J.," I said. "It seems that all I've been doing lately is accidently hitting you with baseballs. It's a good thing *that* one hit you on the head. Otherwise, you might have gotten hurt."

T.J. walked over, shoved me to the ground, and pounced on top of me. "Well, Mr. Skinnybones, we'll just see how good you bunt on Saturday," he said.

"What happens on Saturday?" I asked. But T.J. didn't understand me. It's hard to speak clearly when your mouth is full of someone's leg.

Then I remembered. Saturday was the day when our Little League teams were scheduled to play each other.

chapter eight

Usually, when I go to the Little League field for a game, I don't know who we're going to play until I get there. I just go to the game, lose, and go home. The way I look at it, losing is losing. Who cares who you lose *to*?

A lot of kids don't feel that way. T.J. is one of them. He's one of those kids who *always* knows exactly which team he's playing, and what their record is. Then, a couple of days before they play, he goes around telling the whole world how the other team is going to get creamed. And the trouble is . . . they know it's true.

The day before we played his team, T.J. went all over the playground shouting out that Franklin's Sporting Goods was going to "mop up the

61

floor" with Fran and Ethel's Cleaning Service.

Fran and Ethel's Cleaning Service—that's the name of my team this year. Neat, huh? When I first found out about it, I thought about quitting. But my father explained to me that Fran and Ethel had paid a lot of money to sponsor our team and that it wouldn't be fair if everyone quit just because it was a stupid name.

So far, I've never had a team name that sounded as neat as Franklin's Sporting Goods. Last year my team was called Preston's Pest Control. Our shirts had pictures of little dead bugs all over them. It was really embarrassing.

Anyway, about five minutes after we got to school on Friday, T.J. raised his hand. When the teacher called on him, he stood up.

"I have an important announcement to make," he said. He looked over at me and smiled. "Tomorrow, at 10:30 A.M., my Little League team is going to be playing Fran and Ethel's Cleaning Service. And, since there are two players in this room that will be playing in that game, I just thought that everyone might enjoy seeing it."

Quickly I raised my hand. I just couldn't let T.J. get away with this. My team hadn't won a game all season, and T.J.'s was in first place. It was going to be humiliating.

62

The teacher called on me.

"*I* wouldn't," I said.

"You wouldn't what?" asked the teacher with a puzzled look on her face.

"I wouldn't enjoy seeing it," I answered.

"Then don't come," she said simply.

"Thank you, Mrs. Grayson," I said. Then, I sat down with a big fat smile on my face.

T.J. jumped out of his seat. "He *has* to come, Mrs. Grayson! He's playing in the game! If he doesn't show I'll be the only one from our class playing!"

"Okay, then," I said, after the teacher called on me again, "I guess it's all settled. Since there's only *one* kid from our class playing, all the rest of us will stay home and watch cartoons. Tomorrow, *Wolfman Meets the Super Heroes* is on."

By this time, Mrs. Grayson was pretty confused so she dropped the whole thing. But T.J. didn't. As a matter of fact, he talked about it all day long. After school he even stood at the door as the kids were leaving the classroom. As they passed him, he said, "See you at the big game, tomorrow. Don't forget . . . it starts at 10:30!"

"See you tomorrow, chicken," he laughed as I tried to sneak past him.

"Who are you calling chicken?" I demanded.

T.J. grabbed me by the shirt and pulled me

63

right up to his face. "You. That's who," he said, holding tight.

"I don't mean to be rude, T.J." I said, "but would you mind putting me down? I don't think two people are supposed to be this close unless they're dancing."

T.J. loosened his grip. "Okay, Frankovitch. We'll just see how funny you are tomorrow at the game." Then he smiled and walked away.

Brother, was I ever in for it now! I didn't know what I was going to do. If there's one thing worse than losing, it's losing in front of your whole class.

I've never even played a Little League game in front of a crowd. With a team like mine, you're lucky if even a couple of parents show up. In fact, I hate to admit this, but there are only two people that have shown up at every single game we've played this year . . . Fran and Ethel. They always come to watch us play right after they get off from work. You can tell who they are because they usually stand around wringing out their mops while we warm up.

Anyway, Friday night before the big game, I couldn't sleep at all. I just lay in bed trying to think of a way to get out of playing. I guess I must have thought about it most of the night. But finally, about three o'clock in the morning, I came up with a wonderful idea. I only hoped it would work.

When I went down to breakfast the next morning, I dragged myself into the kitchen on my stomach.

"Good morning, Mom and Dad," I said as I pulled myself over to the breakfast table.

My parents looked down at me on the floor and smiled. "Good morning, Alex," they said together.

"What will you have for breakfast?" asked my mother.

"Cornflakes," I answered, looking up at her.

My mother got up from the table and poured me a bowl of cereal. She stepped over me to get to the refrigerator.

"Juice?" she asked.

I nodded. What was wrong with these people? Didn't they notice that something was wrong with me?

My mother put my breakfast on the floor in front of me. "Better hurry and eat, honey," she said. "You'll have to be dressing for your game soon."

I pushed the cereal and juice out of my way. Then, slowly, I pulled myself over to the table.

When I got there, I pulled my body up into my seat. This whole thing took about ten minutes.

"I think I'd rather eat up here," I said. "Could someone please get me my cornflakes and juice?"

"We're eating right now, Alex," said my dad. "You should have brought your food with you."

Slowly (even slower than before), I leaned down until my hands were on the floor again. The chair flipped over as my body dropped back down. My parents didn't even bother to look up. They were actually ignoring the fact that I couldn't walk!

Finally, I decided to do something really big to get their attention. I pulled myself over to my bowl and started eating my cereal without a spoon. I just put my head in my bowl and started chewing!

After a few minutes of this, my mother walked over to me and dropped a napkin on my head. "You'll probably need this to clean up."

"What kind of parents are you, anyway?" I shouted. "Your poor little son can't walk, and you stand around dropping napkins on his head! Don't you even want to know what happened to me?"

"We already know what happened to you," said my mother calmly.

"You mean that you know about how Ronnie Williams ran over my poor legs with his motor-bike last night? And you know about how they stiffened up while I was sleeping? And about how they won't work anymore?"

"No, Alex," my mom said. "We know that your whole class is going to be at your baseball game today. Dad and I will be there, too. Brian's parents called this morning, and we're going over to the game with them."

"Oh," I said quietly.

I finished my cereal on the floor. Then I silently pulled myself back out of the kitchen and down the hallway to my room. Sometimes, when you're caught doing something dumb, you feel too embarrassed to stop doing it right away.

When I got back to my room, I stood up and took my uniform out of the drawer. I put on the shirt. The neck still hung down to my stomach. This was going to be the worst day of my life.

chapter nine

Finally, I decided to head over to the Little League field. As I got close enough to see the baseball diamond, I noticed something very unusual. All around the field, the bleachers were packed with people. And when I say packed, I mean *packed*!

"Whew!" I said feeling a million times better. "Thank goodness! It looks like the high school must be having their graduation here this morning. It must be some sort of mix-up. Now, I won't have to play after all!"

I jumped high into the air. "Yeehaa!" I screeched. As I turned around to head for home, I noticed that the Channel Six News truck was parked alongside the curb.

68

Wow! I thought to myself. This must really be something *big*. It's even going to be on TV. Then I saw a cameraman get out of the truck.

"Hi," I called to him. "Are you going to put that graduation over there on the news tonight?"

"What graduation?" asked the man. "That's no graduation . . . that's a baseball game."

"A baseball game?" I squeaked.

"Yeah," he continued, "there are two Little League teams playing over there this morning. We're going to film a few minutes of the game to put on the sports news tonight."

"Gee, mister," I said, taking a deep breath. "This must really be an important game to make the weekend sports. What is it . . . the championship or something?"

"Nope," said the cameraman. "It's nothing like that. As a matter of fact, I think that one of these teams I'm going to be filming hasn't won a game all season."

"I'm doomed!" I hollered. Then I flopped down on the curb and put my head in my hands.

"Are you all right?" he asked.

"All right?" I shouted back. "All right? Of course I'm not all right! What kind of man are you anyway, mister? What kind of a person would want to embarrass a poor rotten Little League team by showing it on the six o'clock

69

news? What's wrong with you? Do you get your kicks making fun of little kids, or what?"

"Wait a minute there, son," he said. "Calm down. I didn't come to make fun of anyone. It's the other team we're interested in. The one with T. J. Stoner on it. He's the kid we're doing the story on."

"T.J.?" I asked.

"Yep," he explained. "Yesterday we learned that T. J. Stoner has won every single Little League game he's ever played in. That's a record! In fact, if his team wins today, it will be his 125th straight winning game." I just turned and headed toward the field. As I walked away, the cameraman called after me, "Hey, kid, are you going to be playing in that game?"

"Yeah," I yelled. "I'll be the kid fainting in center field."

What else could go wrong? I looked up into the sky. Maybe now was the time to have a little chat with God. After all, that's what he's there for, isn't it?

"Listen, God," I shouted, "if I did something to make you mad, I'm really sorry. And I'll try never to do it again, whatever it is. But right now, I need your help. I'm a good kid, God. Well . . . pretty good. And I really don't think I deserve

70

this. So I'd like to talk to you about making a little deal.

"If you get all those people sitting in the bleachers to go home right now, I'll become a preacher when I grow up. Would you like that, God?"

I looked around to see if anyone was getting up to leave. No luck. In fact, even more people were coming.

"Okay, God," I said, "if you didn't like that deal, how about this one. All you have to do is get rid of the cameraman. If he goes home, I promise to go to church every single Sunday for the rest of my life."

I looked behind me. The cameraman was carrying all his equipment down to the field. He didn't turn around.

"All right, God," I said one last time. "This is my final offer, and it's a good one. All you have to do is whip up one tiny little thunderstorm to get the game canceled and, in return, I will go home this very minute and read the Bible from cover to cover. How's that?"

I looked into the sky. It was the sunniest, clearest day I had seen in months.

"Thanks, God," I said. "Thanks a whole lot. I know I'm not important like Moses or anything, but I really didn't think it would hurt you to do one tiny little miracle."

When I finally got to the field, my team was already there warming up. Every time I looked into the bleachers my knees turned to jelly. I wasn't sure how long they were going to be able to hold me up.

My coach spotted me.

"Frankovitch," my coach shouted when he spotted me, "where in the heck have you been? Get out there in the field and warm up!"

I trotted out to center field.

"Okay, Alex," he hollered, "I'm going to hit you a couple out there. Get ready."

The first ball he hit me was a high pop fly. I was *very* nervous. It seemed like all the people in the bleachers were staring straight at me.

The ball came fast. I didn't even have time to think about it. I just watched it closely, put out my glove, and made a *perfect* catch!

Hmmm, I thought, maybe this isn't going to be so tough, after all. A crowd might be just the thing I need to bring out the best in me.

"Okay, Alex," shouted my coach, again, "here comes another one."

This time it was a hard grounder. As soon as I saw it coming, I ran up to it, bent down, and scooped it up into my glove.

"All right out there, Frankovitch," yelled the coach. "Way to play!"

Boy, was he ever proud of me! The day was turning out a whole lot better than I thought.

chapter ten

The umpire blew his whistle. It was time for the big game to begin.

Our team ran in from the field. On the sideline T.J. was being interviewed for the six o'clock news. I tried to get close enough to listen to what they were saying, but they had just finished. As T.J. walked off, I heard the newsman say, "Good luck out there today, T.J. We're all rooting for you!"

I looked into the bleachers. On the front row sat Fran and Ethel. They were a little bit hard to spot because they didn't have their mops with them. I smiled to myself. Not *everyone's* rooting for you, T.J., I thought.

The umpire's whistle blew again. "Teams take the field!" he shouted.

T.J.'s team ran out to the field. Naturally, T.J. was pitching. He started warming up and, just like in our contest, every ball he threw went zinging over the plate at about sixty miles an hour. I hate to keep saying this, but he really *was* the best Little League pitcher I had ever seen. I sure was glad I didn't have to be up first.

"Batter up!" shouted the ump.

Kevin Murphy was the first batter on our team. As soon as he stepped up to the plate, I could tell he was really nervous. He kept trying to spit, but nothing would come out. Instead, he just kept making this funny sound with his lips. He looked ridiculous.

When T.J. looked at Kevin, he smiled. Then he wound up and threw the ball as hard as he could. Kevin never even saw it go by.

"Steerrriiiikkkee one!" yelled the umpire.

Kevin looked confused. "Did he already throw one?"

T.J. just laughed and went into his windup for his second pitch. This time he threw it a little bit slower. Kevin swung with all his might. But just as the ball got to the plate, it curved.

"Steerrriiiikkkee two!" screamed the umpire

75

again. Poor Kevin hadn't even come close. I *really* felt sorry for him. Whenever you swing as hard as you can and miss it, you always feel like an idiot. Kevin tried acting tough but, when he went to spit again, he just made that same stupid sound with his lips.

Quickly, he took his bat back and got ready for the next pitch. But unfortunately, the third ball that T.J. threw was even better than the first two. Kevin just watched it go streaking by.

"Strike three! Batter's out!" yelled the ump.

Everyone in the stands began to cheer loudly for T.J. Kevin sat down on the bench and began to cry. He couldn't seem to stop. After a while, his mother had to be called out of the bleachers to get him calmed down. At first the whole team was pretty embarrassed about it. But as it turned out, Kevin was the best batter of the inning. He was the only one who swung.

The second batter, Willy Jenson, didn't even *try* to swing. And by the time the third batter got up, he was so nervous, he didn't even bother to put the bat up to his shoulder. He just stood there, let three pitches go by, and sat down.

Our team was out in the field before we knew it. Everyone was looking pretty sad. What we really needed was a pep talk to get the old team spirit going. So I called all the guys into a huddle.

"Okay, you guys," I said, trying to act real peppy. "All we need to do is hold them. What do you say? Let's get them out one-two-three! Three up. Three down!"

The first baseman looked at me and laughed right out loud. "Frankovitch, you jerk," he said, "who do you think you're kidding? Our team hasn't made three outs in a row all year!"

"Yeah, Alex," said the catcher. "We're lucky if we make three outs the whole game. So why don't you just shut up and get out to center field where you belong?"

So much for the old team spirit. But I didn't care what they said. I was going to cheer our team on, whether they wanted me to or not.

Frankie Rogers was going to be our starting pitcher. As I walked out to center field, I watched him warm up. He threw twice and said he was ready. Frankie doesn't like to warm up for too long. He only throws a couple of good balls a game, and he doesn't want to risk throwing them in practice.

I started cheering. "Okay, Frankie, pitch it in there, babe. Right over the plate, Frankie! You can do it!"

Frankie threw the first ball. It hit the dirt about ten feet in front of the plate.

"Ball one!" shouted the umpire.

77

"That's okay, Frankie, don't worry. You can do it, babe!" I yelled.

All of a sudden Frankie asked the umpire for time-out. Then he turned and walked out toward center field. At first I figured he was probably coming out to thank me for cheering. But when he got close enough, I could see he wasn't smiling. I walked up to meet him.

"Will you please shut up, Alex?" he screamed. "You're really getting on my nerves! How in the world am I supposed to concentrate with all that shouting going on out here?"

"That's not shouting, Frankie, that's cheering!" I told him. "I'm just trying to encourage you a little bit."

"Yeah well, if you ask me, you're acting like a jerk. So how about just shutting up?" Frankie said, stomping back to the pitcher's mound.

As he got ready to throw his next pitch, I yelled, "Okay, Frankie, throw any dumb kind of pitch you want. See if *I* care!"

The ball zoomed toward the plate but, unfortunately, it was just a little bit low. It hit the batter on the foot and he took his base. The next batter hurried up to the plate. Once again, Frankie got ready. This time, he hit the kid at bat in the arm.

If you ask me, he was embarrassing the whole

team. It was bad enough that he couldn't pitch. But to make matters worse, he didn't even throw the ball hard enough to hurt anyone.

I looked over to the sidelines. The news camera was rolling. "Oh no!" I said to myself. I put both my hands over my face so that no one would recognize me on the six o'clock news.

While I was standing there with my face covered up, I heard a big loud crack. I looked up. Some kid had hit the ball and was running to first base.

Everyone began to holler and scream. Then, all the guys on my team turned to look at me. At first I wasn't sure why, so I just sort of smiled. But suddenly I realized that they were watching to see if I was going to catch the ball which was probably headed my way. I panicked. I didn't even know where the ball was! I looked up into the sky to try and find it, but I couldn't see it anywhere! The worst feeling in the world is knowing that any minute a hard ball is going to smack you right in the head, and you don't know where it's coming from.

I had to try to protect myself. Quickly I took my glove off my hand and put it on my head. It was just in time! I felt something hit my glove with a big thud! I felt it roll off the top of my head and land on the ground next to me.

My team started going crazy. "Oh no! He dropped it! He dropped the stupid ball!" they screamed.

"I did not!" I screamed back at them. "How can a person drop something when he didn't even catch it in the first place? Just because something lands on your head does not mean that you caught it!"

"It does too!" shouted the third baseman. "You caught it on your head, and then dropped it!"

"If a bird poops on your head, you don't say that you've caught it, do you, you jerk?" I yelled back.

I was so busy arguing that I forgot all about the ball. By the time I remembered, it was too late. Three runs had already scored.

The coach was waving at me from the sidelines. Just to be polite, I waved back.

"He's not waving, Frankovitch, you jerk," shouted the left fielder. "He's shaking his fists!"

I looked closer. Yup. Those were fists, all right. He was even madder than I thought.

It took a few minutes for things to settle back down. Frankie got ready to face his fourth batter. I looked to see who was up. My heart began to pound.

Slowly T.J. walked up to the plate and took a few practice swings. Then he knocked the dirt off his shoes and pointed to me in center field. My stomach started doing flips. Oh no, I thought to myself. He's going to slam it right to me! Nervously, I backed up. If I made another mistake out there, I was doomed.

Frankie pitched the ball. T.J. pulled the bat back and hit it with all his might. It was a hard grounder, and just as I thought, headed my way!

I watched it as it bounced over second base and started into center field. If only I could remember what the coach had told me about catching hard grounders! If only I could get T. J. Stoner out!

I tried to do everything just like in the big leagues. First, I ran up to meet the ball. Then, I stooped down directly in front of it. I even kept my eye on it. It's almost here! I thought. I've got it! I've got it!

But just as it was about to roll into my glove, it hit a small dirt mound and took a crazy bounce to the right.

"Oh no!" I screamed. I made a diving leap trying to stop it, but it was no use. The ball sped away and kept right on rolling all the way to the back fence.

The crowd went wild. I looked at T.J. as he

was running the bases. He saw me and tipped his cap. What a big shot! He really made me sick!

My coach was screaming for me to get the ball. But I was just too mad. "He hit it!" I hollered, pointing at T.J. "Let *him* go get it!"

Finally, the left fielder went out to retrieve the ball. My coach's face got so red, I could see it from center field. For a minute there, I actually thought he might blow up. Boy, was I in trouble now. I figured it might be a good time to have another little chat with God.

"God, please, whatever you do, don't let our team get up to bat again until my coach settles down. If I have to go over there now, he's going to kill me, God, I know he will. And if you think I'm a problem down here, just imagine what it would be like to have me running around heaven with you. You'd never have a minute's peace, God. Think about it."

Right after I finished talking to God, I watched as Frankie threw nine straight strikes in a row!

"I've done something to upset you, haven't I, God?" I said, looking up to the sky. Then I thought a minute. "If you're still mad about me wearing a gorilla costume in the Christmas play, it wasn't my fault. I told my teacher at least fifty times that I did *not* want to be one of those sheep in the manger."

All the kids on my team were passing me as they headed for the bench. I saw the coach waiting for me on the sideline. He had a very strange grin on his face and kept pounding his fist into his hand. As I walked by, he grabbed my arm and handed me a bat.

I forced a smile. "Someday we'll look back on this and laugh," I said quietly.

"Yeah, Frankovitch," he growled, his teeth clenched together. "You and I are going to do a whole lot of laughing right after the game. But right now you're up. So get your tail over there." Then he gave me a little shove toward home plate.

I dropped my glove on the ground and looked around as I headed toward the batter's box. Sitting in the stands, Fran and Ethel were clapping. Standing on the sideline, the camera-man was filming. And waiting on the mound in front of me, T. J. Stoner was grinning.

This was easily the worst moment of my life. There was no escape. No joke would save me now.

"Get going, Alex!" screamed my coach from behind me.

I gulped and stepped up to the plate. T.J.

began to laugh. Then he turned around and hollered to the rest of his team.

"Easy out! Easy out!" He screamed loud enough for the whole world to hear.

All the guys in the infield took four giant steps in. That didn't do much for my confidence.

"Get ready for a bunt!" yelled T.J.

Oh wonderful! I thought to myself. Now everyone knows exactly what I'm going to do. But I didn't really have a choice. It was either bunt or not hit it at all.

T.J. threw his first pitch. Whoosh! I couldn't believe how fast it came streaking over the plate!

"Steerrriiiikkkee one!" shouted the umpire.

Why do umpires always have to yell "strike" so loud? Whenever it's a ball they practically whisper. But as soon as they see a strike, they act like everyone's deaf or something.

I made up my mind that I wasn't going to just stand there like an idiot and let another ball go by. If I was going to strike out, I was going to do it swinging.

T.J. wound up and threw again. Quickly, I stuck out my bat. As the ball whizzed over the plate, it hit the bat on the corner and began rolling toward first base.

I couldn't believe it. I started running as fast

as I could. If only I could get on base. I'd be a hero! And no one can be mad at a hero. Not even my coach.

The first baseman ran toward me to pick up the ball. Meanwhile, T.J. ran over to cover first.

Everyone was going crazy. My coach was jumping up and down as I passed him running to first. He didn't even look mad anymore. I just had to make it!

The first baseman picked up the ball and got ready to make the throw. I was almost there. Just three more steps to go.

He threw. T.J. got ready for the catch. I had to do something!

"BOOGA BOOGA!" I screamed suddenly, flinging my arms all around. "BOOGA BOOGA!"

T.J. looked surprised. And for just a split second he took his eye off the ball. It shot past him and rolled into the outfield. I WAS SAFE!

As the outfielders scrambled for the ball, I took a chance and headed for second.

"Legs, don't fail me now!" I yelled as I hit full speed. I didn't look back until I was safe at second.

The crowd in the stands went wild.

"I did it! I did it!" I screamed. "A double! I got a double!"

The second baseman told me to shut up. But I ignored him. No one could ruin this moment for me, not the second baseman, not T. J. Stoner, not anyone!

But something didn't look quite right. From second base, I watched as T.J.'s coach ran onto the field and began arguing with the umpire. And before I knew it, my coach was out there, too.

I couldn't figure out what the problem could be. The whole thing was so simple. T.J. had missed the ball and I got a double. A double! Wow! I still couldn't believe it. I started jumping up and down all over again.

Out in the field, my coach had started jumping up and down right along with me. But for some reason he didn't look very happy. All of a sudden, I saw the umpire begin to walk out toward second base.

Don't panic, Alex, I thought. Maybe he's not really coming to second base at all. Maybe during all that excitement, someone threw toilet paper streamers onto the outfield and the umpire's walking out there to clean them up. But in a few seconds, the umpire was standing next to me at second base.

He leaned right down in my face and screamed, "You're out!"

86

"Out?" I asked, puzzled. "How could I be out? I bunted!"

"You interfered with the play at first base," he said.

"I did not!" I argued. "I didn't even touch T.J.!"

"You jumped up and down and shouted 'booga booga,'" said the umpire.

My coach ran up behind the umpire and held out his rule book. "Show me where it says you can't say 'booga booga!'" he demanded. "Tell me, huh? What page is the 'no bogga booga' rule on?"

I don't know why, but suddenly this whole conversation seemed pretty funny. I looked up at the umpire and smiled. "Booga booga," I said quietly.

"Get off the field, you smart aleck," he ordered.

I nodded my head. "Booga," I said again softly.

Then, slowly I began trotting off the field toward the bench. As I was running, I could see T.J. out of the corner of my eye. He had started to laugh. Only I knew he wasn't laughing *with* me. He was laughing *at* me.

I just couldn't let him get away with it. Suddenly, I got an idea. If T.J. wanted to laugh, I might as well give him something to laugh about.

87

Quickly, I changed my direction and began running right toward him. When he looked up and saw me coming, he stopped laughing. I guess he wasn't quite sure what kind of crazy thing I was going to do next.

When I got to the pitcher's mound, I jumped up and down a couple of times, then quickly lifted up his arm and started tickling him. "Booga booga," I said, poking at his ribs.

For the first time in his life, T.J. looked embarrassed. It was great while it lasted, but unfortunately, it didn't last too long. After a couple of seconds he began to look extremely angry. That's when I decided to split.

I ran off the field as fast as I could, and then out the gate. I didn't slow down until I was safely in my own room. Locking the door behind me, I had a feeling that I wouldn't want to come out for a long, long, time.

chapter eleven

I stayed in my room for about an hour before I heard my parents come home from the game. I had pushed my dresser over in front of the door so that no one could get in. I wasn't sure exactly what my father was going to do when he got home, but I had a pretty good idea.

I figured he would probably knock on my door and tell me he wanted to talk to me. When I let him in, he would sit down on the bed and just stare at me for a while. Then he would start one of those big "talks" that parents love to have with their children, and that children hate to have with their parents.

He would start off by telling me that running

away from a problem never solves anything. Then he would say that he hoped I wouldn't keep trying to make a big joke out of everything I'm not good at. And he would end up by telling me that "no matter what you try to do in life, you must always try to do the best you can." Then he would ask me if I understood what he was trying to tell me.

"Yes," I would answer, "I think that you're trying to tell me never to do anything stupid to embarrass the family again."

Then my father would stare at me for a minute, shake his head, and start out of my room. On his way out he would probably mutter something like, "I might as well be talking to a brick wall."

All of a sudden I heard the back door open and close. My heart started to pound. I listened to the sound of Dad's footsteps coming down the hall.

Here it comes, I thought to myself. Next he's going to knock on my door and tell me that he wants to have a little talk.

Knock, knock, knock. . . .

"Who is it?" I asked, as if I didn't know.

"It's Dad."

"Dad who?"

90

"Come on, Alex," said my father. "Open the door. I want to talk to you a minute."

"I already know what you want, Dad," I replied. "You want to talk to me about what happened today. And you probably even think that by talking it out, you can make me feel better. But you might as well save your breath, Dad. It's no use. The way I feel, no one in the whole world could make me feel better. So if you don't mind, I've decided to become a hermit and live right here in my room for the rest of my life. If you or Mom would just shove a bologna sandwich under the door every once in a while, I'd really appreciate it.

"And one more thing, Dad," I added. "Don't try and force your way in here to try and save me. I shoved my dresser up against the door, and I wouldn't want you to hurt yourself."

I figured that by this time, my father was really feeling sorry for me.

"Well, Dad," I said, "it's been real nice having you for a father. I'll see you when I'm all grown-up."

I heard my father leave my door and walk back down the hall toward the kitchen. I knew he was probably going to tell my mother what had happened. Then the two of them would sit down together and try to figure out a way to get me to come out.

A few minutes later, I heard a noise at my door. Aha! I thought to myself. There they are now! They're probably going to stand there and beg me to come out!

But something behind the dresser was making a funny sound. When I looked to see what it was, I saw a bologna sandwich in a plastic bag, being squeezed underneath the space at the bottom of my door.

"Very funny, Dad!" I yelled. "Very, very funny!"

I grabbed the flattened sandwich and threw it in my trash can. Parents! Just when you think you've got them all figured out, they go and pull a dumb trick like that.

The next day was Sunday. And, except for a few minutes while my parents were at church, I didn't come out of my room all day long.

The thing that bothered me most about staying in there all day was that my parents didn't seem to care at all. In fact, every once in a while, I could even hear them laughing. What kind of people think it's funny for a kid to spend the rest of his life shut away in a tiny bedroom?

The other thing that bothered me was how boring it was. Most of the time I just lay on my bed. There were probably better things to be doing, but just in case someone looked through the window to see me, I didn't want it to seem like I was having a good time.

By dinner time, I was really wanting to come out. I could hear my mother starting to make dinner in the kitchen. Boy, was I ever hungry! I had hardly eaten a thing all day.

While my parents were at church I had snuck a few snacks and a couple of apples, but it wasn't nearly enough to keep a growing boy going. Besides, all I had left were two pretzels and one broken graham cracker. I tried putting the pretzels between the graham cracker pieces to make a sandwich, but it looked terrible.

Being hungry wasn't my biggest problem, though. I had to go to the bathroom worse than I've ever had to go in my whole entire life. I waited as long as I could, but finally, I just couldn't stand it one more minute. I pushed the dresser away from the door and ran to the bathroom. I know my parents must have heard me, but no one even bothered to walk down the hall to see how I was. On the way back to my room, I heard them sitting down to dinner. I could smell the delicious aroma all the way down the hall.

I began to wonder how long a person could go without food before he passed out and died. The thought made me very nervous. My stomach started to growl loudly. I decided that maybe if I just got a little peek at some real food, it might make me feel better.

Quietly, I tiptoed down the hall toward the kitchen. Just one little peek . . . that's all I wanted. I stopped at the kitchen door and got down on my hands and knees. Slowly, I peeked around the corner.

Fried chicken and corn on the cob. I just couldn't stand it! My mouth had begun to water so much that I almost started drooling down the front of my shirt.

My parents were staring at me. Neither one of them said anything. They kept right on eating!

"Listen, Mom and Dad," I said, "you might as well forget trying to pretend I'm not here. I know you can see me."

My father looked up. "You're the one who doesn't want anyone to bother you, Alex," he said. "It wasn't our idea."

"Well, maybe I've changed my mind," I said, staring at all the corn on the cob, piled high in a bowl in the middle of the table. Butter was melting down the sides. I sat down in my chair.

"Chicken?" asked my father.

"I am not!" I shouted angrily. "Just because I ran off the Little League field doesn't mean I'm a chicken!"

My father gave me a real disgusted look and then just shook his head. "Chicken?" he said to my mother as he picked up the plate and handed it to her.

"Yes, please," said my mother as she took a big piece of fried chicken off the plate.

My father turned to me and said, "Shall we try it again, Alex? Chicken?" Then he passed me the plate.

I managed to mumble "thank you" but that was the last word I said the entire meal.

My parents tried to talk to me about what happened at the game, but I just couldn't do it. It's bad enough when you act like an idiot, but it's even worse when you have to talk about it.

After dinner, I went back to my room and fed the rest of the graham cracker and the pretzels to my fish. Then I got my pajamas on and went straight to bed. I knew that my parents would make me go to school the next day, and I was going to need a lot of energy to face the kids in my class.

chapter twelve

One of the things I really hate about my mother is that she always seems to know when I'm lying. Don't ask me how she does it. I've tried to figure it out, but so far I've had no luck at all.

On Monday morning, when she came into my room to get me out of bed, I started moaning and groaning and holding my sides.

"Ohhhh . . ." I wailed, "my stomach, my stomach."

My mother rolled up my window shade. "What a nice sunny day out there," she said cheerfully.

"Ohhhh!" I cried loudly, trying to get her attention. "I'm not kidding, Mom. It really hurts! I think I'm dying."

"Okay, Alex," she said standing at the end of my bed with her arms crossed. "If you want me to play this little game with you . . . fine. Now I guess I'm supposed to ask you what's wrong with your stomach."

"Aaggg," I said, doubling over in pain. "It must have been something I ate. Maybe there was something wrong with the chicken I had last night for dinner."

My mother casually strolled over to my dresser and looked down into my fish bowl. "Did your fish have chicken for dinner, too?" she asked.

"Don't try to make me laugh, Mom," I said. "It hurts too much."

"I'm not trying to make you laugh, Alex," said my mother. "Your fish is dead."

"Oh no!" I shouted. I jumped out of bed and ran over to the goldfish bowl. "He's not dead! He can't be!"

"Maybe he's just trying to learn how to float on his back," said my mother with a little laugh.

"How can you make a joke about this?" I hollered.

"Oh, for heaven's sake, Alex," she answered, "you've only had that fish for four days. Your fish never last more than a week. How much can a four-day-old fish mean to you? I would think that by this time, you'd be used to them dying. So far

97

this month, you've already overfed five of them."

"It doesn't matter. I still don't think that you should make fun of someone's pet dying," I insisted.

I got my little fish net and scooped up my dead fish. Then I ran him into the bathroom and flushed him down the toilet. When I got back to my room, my mother was standing there with a smile on her face.

"I see that your stomach is better," she said. "You haven't moaned or groaned for several minutes."

"Ohhhh," I said quickly, grabbing my sides and bending over.

"Forget it, Alex. It won't work. Get dressed. You're going to school," she said, leaving the room.

"I blew it!" I said to myself. I almost had her believing me and I blew it. If it wasn't for that stupid fish, I wouldn't have had to go to school. Boy, you try to do your pet a favor by giving him a special dessert, and this is how he thanks you. He dies. What a pal.

On the way to school, I tried to plan what I would say to the kids when I got there. I knew that everyone was going to be making fun of the way that I had acted at the game. And what made it even worse was that I also knew that T. J. Stoner was going to be the big fat hero.

As I got near the playground, I could already see about a million kids gathered around T.J. They were asking him for his autograph! All those jerky kids were actually asking T. J. Stoner for his autograph!

I rushed by in a hurry to get to my classroom. Luckily, no one saw me. I figured that if I could just get to my desk before class started, no one would have a chance to make fun of me.

I was wrong. When I walked into the classroom, my teacher looked up and started to giggle. "Ooga ooga," she said.

I frowned. "It wasn't 'ooga, ooga,' Mrs. Grayson," I said disgustedly. " 'Ooga ooga' is the sound an old-fashioned car makes. What I *said* was, 'booga booga.' "

"Oh," she said quietly, looking a little embarrassed. "It was hard to hear you from the stands."

"Mrs. Grayson, I was wondering if I could sit in the back of the room today?" I asked. "I'm feeling a little sick and I might need to run to the bathroom from time to time."

Before Mrs. Grayson had a chance to answer me, the bell rang and everyone started rushing in to take their seats.

"Hey, look who's here," shouted T.J. "It's Booga Booga Frankovitch!" The whole class started laughing at once.

"Would you like to go to the nurse?" Mrs. Grayson shouted over the laughter.

"No thanks," I yelled even louder. "If I feel like I'm going to toss my cookies, I'll just aim for T.J. He's a pretty good catch."

"What a threat!" laughed T.J. "If you toss your cookies like you toss a baseball, you'll miss me by a mile."

"That's enough," said Mrs. Grayson, motioning for both of us to sit down.

I was glad she stepped in. For the first time in my life, I didn't have anything else to say.

T.J. raised his hand. "Mrs. Grayson," he said after he was called on, "would it be all right if I finished signing a couple of autographs for some of the kids in the room? I didn't have a chance to finish before class."

Mrs. Grayson smiled. "Sure, T.J.," she answered. "I think we can spare a few minutes to let the National Little League Champion sign a few autographs."

Everyone started clapping. I couldn't believe it! You might have thought he was Tom Seaver or something!

"Boys and girls," said Mrs. Grayson, "I really think that we're very fortunate to have T.J. in our room this year. In case any of you missed it on the news Saturday night, T. J. Stoner is going to be in the *Guinness Book of World Records*! He now holds the record for the most games ever won in a row in the history of Little League baseball!"

More applause.

I couldn't stand it one more minute. Quickly I got out my notebook and scribbled a message to Brian. It read:

"Say something nice about me and I'll give you a dollar after school."

Brian's hand shot up in the air like a bullet. Brian loves money more than any kid I know.

"Yes, Brian?" said Mrs. Grayson.

"Mrs. Grayson," he began, "I think we're also fortunate to have Alex Frankovitch in our class this year. If you ask me, it takes a very special person to stand in front of a crowd and make a big buffoon out of himself like Alex did."

This time even Mrs. Grayson couldn't keep from laughing. When I become popular, I think Brian will be the first friend I'll dump.

The rest of the day I tried to stay as quiet as I could. I wanted to make it as easy as possible for people to ignore me. But it didn't work. All day long, whenever anyone walked by my desk, they would lean over and whisper 'booga booga' in my ear as they passed. Then they'd walk away and laugh as if they were the first one to think of it.

By one o'clock I just couldn't take it one more second. That's when Harold Marshall raised his hand and asked if he could sharpen his pencil. Harold's a troublemaker, so he has to ask permission to do anything.

Mrs. Grayson nodded her head and Harold started up my row to the pencil sharpener. I was positive that when he passed my desk he would try to get in a couple of quick boogas. So as he got closer to my seat, I got ready for him.

Just as Harold leaned over to whisper in my ear, I quickly turned my face in his direction, making it look as if he had just leaned over and kissed me.

I jumped up. "Yuck! Did you see that?" I yelled wiping off my face. "Harold Marshall just kissed me on the cheek! How revolting!"

Harold started turning red. "I did not!" he sputtered.

"Then how did my cheek get so wet?" I asked

pointing to my face. "Mrs. Grayson, can I go to the bathroom and wash it off? I think I'm allergic to slobber."

Mrs. Grayson motioned me out the door and ordered Harold to sit down. As I left the room, I saw several kids covering their faces as Harold passed by.

Unfortunately, making a fool out of Harold didn't really change anything. As soon as I got back from the bathroom, the booga boogas started all over again.

I looked at the clock. Only forty-five minutes to go. I just didn't know if I could make it that long. I began feeling sorry for myself. It seemed like nothing I had ever done had turned out right. Even when I did something well, like bunting for instance, it turned out wrong.

"Let's face it Alex," I finally said to myself, "the only thing that you've ever really succeeded at is being short. You're a nothing. A big fat nothing!"

I leaned my head down and rested it on my desk. I felt my eyes starting to get wet. Oh terrific! I thought. Now big fat nothing Alex Frankovitch is going to cry in front of the whole class.

Suddenly, I heard my name being called. I

didn't look up. "*Alex Frankovitch?*" said the voice again. But it wasn't my teacher. Quickly I wiped a tear out of my eye and looked up. The voice was coming from the loudspeaker on the wall.

It was our principal, Mr. Vernon. "*Mrs. Grayson, is Alex Frankovitch there?*" he asked.

"Yes he is, Mr. Vernon," she answered. "Would you like me to send him down to your office?"

"*No,*" said Mr. Vernon. "*I have an announcement to make about him and I just wanted to be sure that he was there.*"

My heart started beating wildly. T.J. pointed at me and started to laugh. We both figured we knew what was coming. Mr. Vernon was going to make a couple more booga-booga jokes so the whole school could have a good laugh.

Mr. Vernon clicked on the loudspeaker so that all the other classrooms could hear him.

"*Attention, boys and girls, may I have your attention, please?*

"*First of all, I'd like to congratulate T. J. Stoner on his brilliant Little League performance! The entire school is very, very proud of him. I think that we should all give him a big round of applause!*"

Then he stopped a minute so that all the classrooms could clap.

"*By the way,*" he continued, "*I have already spoken to T.J. today, and he has agreed to stay after school in case any of you would like to stop by and get his autograph. We'll have a table set up for him in the Multipurpose Room.*"

T.J. just sat there and grinned like a big shot. I wished I had my dead fish back. I would have put it down his shirt.

"*Now then,*" Mr. Vernon's voice came back through the loudspeaker. "*There's someone else in Mrs. Grayson's sixth-grade room that I'd also like to congratulate.*"

Here it comes, I thought to myself. He's going to congratulate me for being the biggest buffoon in the school.

"*It seems that Alex Frankovitch has also made quite a name for himself.*"

I could feel everyone's eyes staring at my back. A few kids were already giggling. Tears started to fill my eyes again, but I forced them back into my head.

"*I have just received news from his mother, that today Alex Frankovitch got a letter in the mail announcing that he is the winner of the National Kitty Fritters Television Contest! And according to the letter, as his prize, Alex will get to appear in a national television commercial!*

"Congratulations, Alex! We're all very excited about having one of our students become a big TV star!"

The whole class was completely silent. No one could believe what Mr. Vernon had said. Especially me! I only wrote that letter as a joke!

After a few seconds I guess the shock wore off, and everyone started clapping. Mrs. Grayson told me to stand up and take a bow, but my legs were so weak I couldn't get out of my chair. So I just turned around and waved instead.

Just then, my mother appeared in the doorway. Mrs. Grayson went to greet her and called me to the front of the room.

"How was that for a big surprise?" asked my mother when she saw me. "I was going to tell you in person, but I happened to see Mr. Vernon on the way down the hall, and we decided it might be more fun to surprise you with it over the loudspeaker. Were you surprised?"

I nodded. Up until this time, I had been unable to say anything. It's hard to form words when your mouth is hanging wide open.

"When do you get to do the commercial?" asked Mrs. Grayson.

"I'm not sure," I said finally, trying to think back to the instructions on the contest sheet. "I just entered that contest as a joke," I admitted. "I didn't really pay much attention to the prize."

My mother waved a piece of paper in front of my face. "It says here that the commercial will be made in New York sometime within the next six months!" she said proudly. "They also said that your contest entry was the funniest, most original essay that they had ever received. And they can't wait to meet you!"

Mrs. Grayson put her hand on my shoulder. "This might just be your start in show business!" she said. Then she and my mother both laughed.

Well I hate to tell them, but they just might be right. Once those Kitty Fritters people get a hold of me, they'll probably never want to let me go. I smiled at the thought of it.

After a few more minutes, my mother left the classroom and went home. Since the day was almost over, Mrs. Grayson told us to put all our work away.

"I just got a great idea," she said. "Why don't we have our two class celebrities come up here and answer questions like they do on TV?"

Since I was already in the front of the room, I casually got up from my seat and sat down on the front edge of Mrs. Grayson's desk. T.J. was a little slower getting there. But finally he shuffled up and sat down next to me. I could tell he really hated sharing his big day with me.

"Okay," said Mrs. Grayson. "Who has questions?"

Harold Marshall's hand was up like a bullet.

"Yes, Harold?" said T.J. quickly.

Harold stood up. "I have a question for Alex," he said, laughing. T.J. smiled. I was sure he already knew what Harold was going to ask. They had probably set it up before T.J. came to the front of the room.

"What exactly is a booga booga?" he asked, cracking up.

I knew it! I knew he was going to say something like that!

I thought a minute before I answered. "It's hard to explain," I said after a minute. "A booga booga is sort of a big wad of green slimy . . . wait a minute! What a coincidence! If everyone will turn around quickly, there's a booga booga sitting in Harold's hair right now!"

Everybody started laughing all at once. Everybody except Harold, that is. Mrs. Grayson didn't seem to mind. I guess she knew that Harold deserved it.

After that, Harold didn't give me any more trouble and T.J. and I started answering questions. Melissa Phillips asked each of us who our most famous relative was. T.J. said it was his brother, Matt Stoner. I said it was my grandmother, Steve Garvey.

Most of the questions were about the *Guinness Book of World Records*. But I didn't really mind. It felt good just sitting up there.

I looked over at T.J. as he answered a question from Adam Brooks. T.J. was a creep all right. But maybe it wasn't all his fault. I had a feeling that being a big shot can make a creep out of anyone if they're not careful. Even a wonderful guy like me. Maybe I better not dump Brian after all, I thought to myself. It might be bad for my image.

"That's all we have time for today," said Mrs. Grayson. "If we have any free time tomorrow, we can continue."

I went to my desk and picked up my homework books. After the bell rang, I filed out of the room with everyone else. As I passed by Mrs. Grayson, she patted me on the back. Maybe after all these years I'd finally done it. Maybe I'd finally found a teacher who liked my sense of humor.

Outside the building, Brian was waiting for me. When he saw me coming, he smiled. I didn't.

"Oh no you don't," I said. "Just because I'm famous and popular doesn't mean you can come crawling back to me. I'm not forgetting how you called me a buffoon."

Brian got a puzzled look on his face. "What are you talking about, Alex?" he asked. "Who's crawling back? I'm just waiting to collect the buck you promised me for saying something nice."

"You call buffoon, nice?"

"I didn't call you a buffoon, Alex," he corrected. "If I had called you a buffoon I would have only charged you fifty cents. I called you a *big* buffoon. That's a dollar. You get twice the buffoon for your money."

I couldn't keep myself from laughing. It's hard to stay mad at Brian. We started walking home together. As we walked, a couple of kids congratulated me on the TV commercial. No one asked for an autograph, but I figure that will probably come later.

On the way home, Brian and I talked a lot about my future as a comedian. We decided that as long as I've already gotten my first break into show business, I might as well go on to become disgustingly rich. I told Brian that I would think about letting him write some of my material. "Material" is the word comedians use when they talk about their jokes.

110

I still can't get over it. Me, skinny little Alex Frankovitch, a star. Hmm. I wonder if the Kitty Fritters people will want me to read my winning essay on the commercial. No, they'll probably just want to use my cute little face smiling at a cat food bag or something. I just hope they don't want me to do anything dumb. Sometimes these commercials can get pretty crazy.

One time I saw a cereal commercial where they made this little kid dress up like a raisin and dance around a big bowl of oatmeal. Boy, the thought of doing something like that really gives me the creeps. Hmm. Maybe it's time for another little chat.

"Hello, God? It's Alex Frankovitch again. Listen, I have another little favor I'd like to ask. As you probably know I'm going to be on a TV commercial soon. And well, I'd *really* appreciate it if I didn't have to dress up like a Kitty Fritter and dance around a cat dish. I mean, I don't mind making a fool of myself once in a while, God. But I do have my pride.

"Are you listening, God? If you are, please just do me this one little favor, and I promise to stop singing 'doo-da' at the end of the hymns in church, and start singing "Amen" like everyone else. How's that? Is it a deal, God? If it is, show me by making the wind start blowing.

111

"Aha! I saw it. I saw a little leaf move on that tree over there. Thanks a lot, God! I *knew* I could count on you.

"And remember, if you ever need a favor, you can count on me, too. Just look me up in New York or Hollywood.

"I'll be in the *Yellow Pages* under 'Star.' "

DESDEMONA-
Twelve Going on Desperate

DESDEMONA-
Twelve Going on Desperate

by Beverly Keller

Lothrop, Lee & Shepard Books
New York

6   7   8   9   10

Library of Congress Cataloging-in-Publication Data
Keller, Beverly.   Desdemona, twelve going on desperate.
Summary: Calamity stalks a seventh grader in the form of social disasters, and
throughout it all, to her great embarrassment, she keeps running into the most
attractive boy in school. [1. Single-parent family—Fiction. 2. Schools—Fiction.
3. Humorous stories] I. Title.   PZ7.K2813De   1986   [Fic]   86-10655
ISBN 0-688-06076-5

To Dulce

one

Bramwell Grove started destroying my life before I ever met him.

It began with a morning telephone call in early November. My father left the twins and me at the breakfast table while he went to answer it.

"That was Harley Grove," he said when he came back. "He wants to bring his brother Bramwell over to see our house."

The twins were too young to be interested, but I was puzzled. "Why would our landlord want to show his brother our house?"

My father looked the way he does when the car's engine makes a new and sinister sound he can barely hear. "I don't know, Dez. Something's going on, though. I put him off until after I get back from the mental health convention, but I want you all to come right home from school today and clean your room. It's going to take a week to make this house fit to see."

Mrs. Farisee, our housekeeper, set a platter of

1

pancakes down so hard the table shivered. She gazed at my father silently. Mrs. Farisee is twenty pounds heavier and at least twenty years older than he, and her stare would make a barbarian tremble.

She had a right to be offended. Mrs. Farisee's attitude toward dirt and dust and clutter is "No quarter!" She kept the ancient stove and linoleum and our battered furniture polished, but she considered anything lurking in the yard or under our beds beyond her jurisdiction.

"I mean general repairs," my father murmured hastily, "all the things I've been meaning to get around to."

When he left for work, he looked worried. He had reason, considering the condition of our house.

Mrs. Farisee was rebuttoning my brother's coat when Sherman Grove came to walk us to school.

Before he had started kindergarten, Antony took his clothes off publicly whenever he felt at odds with things. In a few weeks, the education system had civilized him so that he only buttoned his coat wrong every morning. I couldn't help feeling a little sad that he'd given in so easily.

The school had put Antony in morning session and Aida in afternoon, I suppose on the theory that twins can become over-dependent on each other.

It was true that my brother and sister had never been very interested in other people. Since they understood each other without speaking, they had a full social life without anybody else.

2

My father was afraid the forced separation might make them more dependent on each other out of school, but he didn't argue with the administration. "They probably buy the myth that a psychologist's kids have more problems than most," he said. "If I try throwing my weight around, they'll start looking for quirks in my kids."

So I walked Antony to school in the morning and walked Aida home in the afternoon.

Sherman, of course, walked with me both ways. Except for sleeping at home, he spent most of his free time with my family.

It hadn't been easy starting junior high only months after we moved to this town. It seemed as if all the other girls in the school had known one another from birth. I didn't understand their jokes, and I was sure I didn't dress right, and I was worried about acting so friendly I'd seem desperate or so cool I'd seem snobbish. While a few girls talked to me, none had ever asked me over or walked home with me or sat with me at lunch.

Being new in junior high is like being the sister of twins, circling people who are in a huddle, getting only a glimpse over their shoulders now and then.

It didn't do me any good socially to be trailed everywhere by my landlord's eleven-year-old son, a loner who was widely regarded as a wimp.

Sherman was also the best friend I'd ever had. When I was sick with the flu, he lugged his VCR all the way to our house, with his favorite tapes. It takes a lot of devotion for an eleven-year-old to let himself be seen in public pulling a red wagon.

I owed Sherman more than that. When his father found out we had three dogs and gave us an eviction notice, it was Sherman who saved us. At the town's big Founder's Day picnic, he managed to get lost. My father and Shirley Miller and I found Sherman, and even had our pictures in the paper with the caption *Rescuers of Grove Boy*. While Harley Grove could hardly evict us after that, he rented to us grudgingly. Knowing Sherman was kind of like having a friend at court. How could I tell him he was a social catastrophe?

We had to wait while Mrs. Farisee made Antony take off his rain boots and put them on the proper feet. Then he and Sherman and I hurried out the door.

It's a comfort to have anybody, *anybody,* to walk with when you're afraid you're late for school.

Even at twelve and a half, with years of on-time attendance behind me, I remembered how it felt to walk to school late and alone. I doubt if anyone ever forgets completely.

Your parents go to bed without setting the alarm, or without changing the clock for daylight saving time, or the broken shoelace you'd tied together breaks again with no room for another knot, or you spill juice down your sweater, or you can't find your books.

The worst, the very worst, is when your parents

4

know you're so late they don't even try to rush you. Grim, deadly calm, they make you sit down and try to eat breakfast.

By the time you dash out the door, you're terrified. Running, you start to have delusions. You imagine that it's not really that late, that in another block you'll see other kids headed for school. But your stomach knows.

You strain for the sight of even one other wretched straggler, but you know you are so late you'd be better off going home. You can imagine walking home, but you can't imagine actually walking in the door. *And what if your parents forced you to walk right back to school, alone, and later than anybody had ever been?*

Just remembering made me walk faster. Sherman and Antony hurried to keep up with me.

Then we saw some kids ahead of us, ambling along and goofing around, and more coming down the side streets.

Now that I knew we weren't late, I slowed down, so we wouldn't catch up with anybody walking to junior high. Being in the company of a kindergartner and a seventh-grader who looked young for his age, the last thing I wanted was to be noticed.

The dozen blocks from our house to the grade school were like an introduction to the town. A block after the street where we lived, the houses were bigger than ours, some with newer paint, but all with single-car garages. A couple of blocks after that, the houses were bigger yet, and some drive-ways had a car *and* a camper in them. Then we came to the streets where the houses had two-car garages and the people kept their vehicles inside, so there were no oil stains on the driveways.

Along the street to our right, the front yards were wide and deep. I'd walked down there once or twice, all the way to where the yards had curved drive-ways and gardeners with leaf blowers tidying the lawns.

Mike Harbinger lived in that neighborhood. On my way to school I'd sometimes see him coming down the street with his friends, a gaggle of little kids tagging after them.

I would have planned my mornings around not letting Mike Harbinger see me with Sherman, ex-cept that I knew Mike Harbinger would not see me if I wore sparklers between my teeth. At fifteen, Mike was over six feet tall and not even gangly. He had thick blond hair and brown eyes, he'd never worn braces, and nobody knew anybody who'd ever seen him with a pimple. I knew a lot about him just from listening to other girls. If you were anywhere around junior high school girls, you couldn't avoid hearing about him. He'd been on the honor roll ever since grade school. He was the high school's best hope for the next four years in basketball, football, and track.

Even girls who looked old enough to be high school sophomores hung around the football field after school watching him at practice.

6

A few times, when Sherman had a cold or stayed after school to work on a project, I walked Aida home by way of the football field. She didn't even complain until we dawdled down to barely moving.

If Mike was aware of all the attention he attracted, he never acted like it. Maybe he'd been admired so long he'd just stopped noticing. He might not have realized how many girls were watching him, since two or three of the guys he hung out with were almost as gorgeous as he. The rest of his friends ranged from good athletes with average looks to a couple of guys who couldn't make it to school without tripping on the curbs.

While Mike Harbinger was clearly out of reach, a few super-popular girls in my school, like Marti Dunnigan and Kerri White, didn't let reality discourage them. Every morning at our lockers they went through the same breathless routine: "Did you see him? Did you see him look at me? Didn't he?" "I know! I know! I think he looked at me, too!"

This morning there was no sign of Mike or his crowd, and I knew I wasn't late for school, so I was able to think of other things. "Your dad called my father this morning," I told Sherman. "He wants to bring your uncle over to see our house. Why, do you suppose?"

"Because he's up to no good, that's why."

Sherman is brilliant, in his own way. He's interested in a great range of things. None of them seemed likely to enhance his social life. His room was full of state-of-the-art electronics and volumes

7

on ecology, archeology, and geology—even his father's outdated real estate manuals and books like *Dress for Success* and *How to Be Your Own Best Friend.*

"When your landlord shows somebody the place you're renting," he went on soberly, "it means he wants to sell it or move in himself. Nobody in my family would live in a dump like yours, and anybody who bought it would either raise the rent or have some kind of deal going. My uncle wouldn't piddle around with buying one crummy house at a time. That means there's something in the works."

Right away, I felt that old rock in my stomach, a mossy boulder sitting in a dank, chill cave. As we crossed the street, I took Antony's hand. "That means I should worry, right?"

"It means that if my Uncle Bramwell buys, you're out." Sherman reached for Antony's other hand. "You could leave the house a mess, but that would be risky. If Bramwell didn't buy it, my father might blame you. He only lets you stay with the dogs because you and your dad—and Shirley Miller—had your picture in the paper the time you found me after I got lost." Sherman always paused a moment after he said "Shirley Miller." Shirley was over thirty, not flashy or beautiful. She had a fine face, though, lean, with clear tanned skin and white even teeth and green eyes with little laugh crinkles at the corners. She was tall and thin, and she moved like a dancer or a runner. The best thing about Shirley was that you knew she acted how she really was: honest and funny and very smart. When we found Sherman, it was Shirley who had scrambled down into the gulley and boosted him up to my father and me.

Poor Sherman, in love with his best friend's father's girl.

"My father couldn't throw you out after that without looking tacky," Sherman went on. "To people like my parents, looking tacky is almost as bad as losing money. So if the place is such a mess my uncle doesn't buy it, my father will be stuck with it, and then he'll be sure to kick you out."

I stopped, not even caring who saw us. "Wait a minute. What about looking tacky?"

"It's been months since you guys rescued me. Did you think he'd be grateful forever?"

As we neared the grade school, Antony watched the kindergarten kids running and talking and laughing. He freed his hands from ours, but he stayed close beside me.

"The other possibility," Sherman said thoughtfully, "is that if the place looks as bad as usual, Bramwell will talk my father into lowering the price, buy it, and kick you out. Tacky would not bother my uncle."

We entered the grade school grounds, Antony so close to me I was in danger of tripping over him. I took him to the door, as I did every morning. "Be sure to come right home," I told him.

He nodded, and trudged through the door by himself.

For a minute, I wondered if Antony and Aida and I were doomed to be social disasters forever. But I had more urgent worries. As Sherman and I headed for our junior high, I asked, "Why would your uncle want a two-bedroom cottage with one bathroom and worn-out linoleum? You said he doesn't fool around with one crummy house at a time."

"Remember when Mr. Troup put his house up for sale and my father tried to buy it? After my father finally agreed to pay the asking price, Mr. Troup decided not to sell. He said that if my father agreed to pay full price for anything, there had to be some deal in the works, and he wasn't going to budge until he found out what. My dad was furious."

According to Sherman, Eleazar Troup attended City Council meetings solely for the chance to call Harley Grove a slumlord in public. "What did your father ever do to him?"

Sherman slowed down a little. "Nothing, so far. I think it's ... I don't know. Maybe it's a matter of style. My dad's young, with all his hair and teeth and muscles. He jogs and plays tennis and he looks great. Even his shirts are made to order. He was elected to the City Council on his first try. We live in a big house, and we have two new cars. Mr. Troup is old and shriveled and he walks as if his bones hurt. His house is all he owns in the world. My mom is always mentioned in the society pages, and his only kid is a reporter on a dumb local newspaper."

I didn't point out that the society pages were in the same local newspaper. I could see what Sherman meant, though. If you had an only child who was a surgeon or a judge, you'd have at least some reflected sense of importance. Personally, I thought it would be more interesting to be a reporter, but there aren't many rich, famous reporters outside of television.

"My father says Pat Troup is the best newsperson in the state," I observed.

My father didn't really know Pat Troup—just enough to say hello when he happened to see her coming to or from her dad's. She was in her early twenties, not much over five feet tall, with a round face and big, nearsighted dark brown eyes. The plastic lenses of her heavy-rimmed glasses were always scratched, and everything I'd ever seen her wear looked left over from Dr. Who's garage sale. Even her short, black curly hair looked like Dr. Who's.

Pat's father wasn't on speaking terms with any of my family. When we first moved in, he made it clear he was dubious about having children and animals next door. Of course, there's a built-in probability that three kids and three dogs are going to do things to upset a less-than-friendly neighbor. I suspect we were much of the reason he put his house up for sale.

My father tried to tell us Mr. Troup was selling because he didn't need the space after Pat got married. She had a big wedding, but a few weeks later,

Cheryl Fabares, who had been a high school class-mate of Pat's new husband, Sonny, came back for a visit. Cheryl had been a pom-pom girl and high school homecoming queen and a junior fashion model at Lowering's Department Store downtown.

A few days after Cheryl arrived, Sonny told Pat their marriage had been a mistake.

After the divorce, Pat lost a lot of weight, and was shifted to writing obituaries, probably because she had started crying at awkward times. Lately she'd gained back her weight and was covering the news again, but she didn't move home with her father.

I knew the whole story just from overhearing talk around the school lockers. Some of the girls had big sisters who actually knew the people involved per-sonally. The story had passion, betrayal, shame, everything. "She should have known, marrying a younger man," Marti Dunnigan said solemnly. Kerri White pointed out that Sonny was only a couple of years younger than Pat, but everybody around the locker sided with Marti, probably be-cause that made it all the more poignant. Teena Brannigan, who had the lead in the first school play of the season, kept saying, "She must be devas-tated."

I was impressed, myself, with how brave Pat was to stay in town and keep working on the paper when she knew everybody was feeling sorry for her or saying she should have known better than to marry a younger man.

I could feel for Mr. Troup, too. It must hurt to see your grown child suffering when she's too old to cry on your lap.

As we walked in the front door of our school, I thought about my own family's problems again. "Sherman, it sounds to me as if, no matter what we do, we're likely to end up with no place to live."

"Well . . . whatever happens, you get thirty days' notice. That's the law." He turned down the left-hand corridor to his locker.

I knew, of course, he'd find me at lunch, just as I knew he'd walk home with Aida and me. This day, though, I was grateful. So long as Sherman kept analyzing the problem, it kept me busy thinking about it, rather than simply fretting.

There's hardly a minute or a place in junior high school that doesn't relate to your social status.

Lunchtime sums it all up. At the peak of security are the people who know beforehand not only with whom they'll sit, but where. Each table is like a separate colony, with some clustered like federations. If I had the nerve, I would make this observation in social studies.

There are the tables where the most popular people sit, and the tables taken by the fairly popular, and tables where people stick together out of self-protection. Then there are outskirt tables, with a lot of empty seats.

There are rules for lunchtime loners. You never

13

sit at a table occupied by people who always eat together. You avoid tables with couples who look as if they want to be left alone. When you pick a table, you leave at least one empty chair on either side of you so nobody will think you're pushy.

When Sherman got to lunch ahead of me, he had no trouble saving me a seat. When he arrived after me, there was always an empty chair next to me.

If Sherman had already found a table, he'd wave to me, and I'd go sit with him. You can't ignore somebody who has saved you a seat and is frantically waving. Besides, if I did, he'd probably come to wherever I was sitting and ask why I was mad.

This day, I looked for him as I entered. All morning, I'd been thinking about how much trouble we had had finding a place to rent when we'd moved to town. Then, when Mr. Grove was going to evict us, my father had spent every weekend and evening searching for another place that would take three children and three dogs.

He never found one.

I joined Sherman at a table where two other people were trying to look absorbed in what they were eating.

I could always tell the mood of the Groves' maid by the lunches Sherman brought. New maids usually packed him sandwiches with the crust trimmed off, the tomatoes sliced thin, olives or pickles drained and isolated in foil or leakproof bags, cakes or pastries in little plastic boxes, and maybe a thermos full of soup or hot chocolate.

14

Their current maid's morale was falling. On Monday, he'd brought hors d'oeuvres, mixed nuts, and garnishes left over from his parents' weekend entertaining. Tuesday, she sent him to school with a lunch of leftover clam dip and no chips.

I unwrapped my sandwich. "There could be some other reason your father wants to show your uncle our house."

"I hope so, Dez."

"I guess the safest thing to do is fix up the place, though."

"I guess." Here it was near the end of the week, and instead of pickles or olives with his sandwich, Sherman had four cocktail onions, stained in various pastel shades where the party toothpicks had been stuck in them.

"Besides," I said, "my father will see that we do." The more I talked, the more depressed I felt.

"You want my cashews?" Sherman asked.

I shook my head.

two

Sherman never waited for me at my locker after school. I think he found Kerri and Marti overwhelming. Besides having skipped a grade, he was small for his age, and they towered over him.

He was waiting at the exit this afternoon, as usual.

We walked to Aida's school. She came out alone, in the wake of clusters of laughing, talking little girls.

"You want to come by my house?" Sherman asked after we'd all walked a block. "I taped Bruce Springsteen's new video."

Aida looked up at me, but I said, "We can't. The house, remember?"

"Probably the best video he's ever made," Sherman said.

"Well . . . just to see that one. Then we've got to get home and start working."

16

Sherman was right. It was a great video. Afterward, he played a whole string of Springsteen videos, from the concert clip of "Rosalita," before The Boss had muscles, through the ones where he got older and stronger. Even a strange, wimpy kid like Sherman can understand what this macho-looking, New Jersey–talking guy is singing about. My sister understood that "Born in the U.S.A." and "My Hometown" were very serious. She watched solemnly and respectfully.

By the time I remembered we were supposed to go right home from school, I had to run all the way, dragging poor Aida, furious with myself for getting us into trouble.

Though Mrs. Farisee was grim, she wasted only a few minutes castigating us. Antony had already hauled a great pile of junk out from under the bunk bed, and Aida and I went to work, chastened.

One thing about Mrs. Farisee, she dealt with a situation when it came up, rather than save it for our father. She didn't mention anything about our being late when he got home for dinner.

By the time I'd finished my homework that evening, he had cleaned the kitchen and bathroom grouting and reattached a sofa arm. He was beginning to replace the broken light switch inside the front door.

I held the flashlight for my father and told him about Sherman's analysis of why Harley Grove wanted to show Bramwell Grove our house.

"The kid's fantastic," my father said, lining up the switch plate.

"You mean he's right?"

"I have lived in rentals most of my life. I can guarantee you he's right." He screwed the plate onto the wall.

"He's not even twelve yet."

"He watches. He listens. He's an outsider." My father tested the new switch, and it worked.

"He is also generally known as a wimp."

My father sat on the sofa, careful not to lean on the arm. "I'm sure he is. I'm willing to bet that nobody comes looking for his company, or chooses him for a team, or asks his opinion. If his parents listened when he yowled in his crib, they haven't heard him since. He has time to watch and think without anybody tampering with his ideas."

Our dog Sadie got up and strolled over to lean against my father's leg. He scratched her behind the ears absentmindedly. "Fortunately, Sherman is a gentle soul. A highly intelligent wimp who cherishes grievances or has a brittle conscience means big trouble. If he goes establishment, he sits at a big table advising others how to inflict maximum casualties on an enemy or a competitor."

Herb and Joe, our male dogs, crowded in between Sadie and my father. Dogs don't waste time fussing. Sadie came and sprawled across my legs, now that I was lying on the floor.

My father scratched Herb and Joe around their necks. "If we're luckier than we deserve, wimps

18

grow up to produce harmless and dazzling technologies or theories or cures, and all the jocks and cheerleaders who ignored them pretend they were their best friends in school."

He stopped scratching. Herb and Joe gave him a minute to start again. When he didn't, they came and flopped down by me. Herb rested his head on Sadie's side, and Joe planted his great paws across my feet.

All three dogs are large and shaggy and prone to shedding. Herb looks like an Old English sheepdog, with some Labrador retriever and beagle thrown in. Joe seems to be mainly Newfoundland, with a bit of collie and Belgian sheepdog. Sadie may well be a mix of vizsla, German shepherd, and Gordon setter. Whatever they are, they're sociable, even when they're not moving.

It's comforting to be around mellow animals and a parent in a conversational mood.

"Steven Spielberg was a wimp in high school," my father said. "So was Stephen King, which is undoubtedly where he got stories like *Carrie*. So was Bruce Springsteen."

I sat up. I love my father. I respect my father. But there are some things you cannot accept, even from a parent. "No. No. Not Bruce Springsteen. Bruce Springsteen was never a wimp."

"I read it somewhere. He said he was really out of it all through high school. What do you think his song 'Glory Days' is all about? It's about those high school cheerleaders and baseball stars passing

19

thirty, selling cars or working in little offices, and dreaming of their glory days, or of lives like the wimps have made for themselves."

Being a psychologist, my father studied these things. Being a psychologist instead of a psychiatrist, he works for salary in a little office at an underfunded community health clinic. He was a marriage counselor before my mother walked out on us. He lost a lot of clients then, and, before he got the job he has now, he sold cars for a while.

For a second, I thought that if he'd ever seen the video he'd know it was about a high school baseball player who ends up a construction worker. Then I realized that even if he'd seen the video, which wasn't likely, the song would still be, to him, about the kind of dead end closest to him. That's why he hadn't mentioned any female wimps.

From what he'd told me about his high school days, my father hadn't been totally out of it, but I knew without asking that his glory days, however long gone, had never been that great.

He is over forty, and the Springsteens and Spielbergs and Kings had been freshmen when he was a graduating senior.

I sat there, my legs pinned down by dogs, and wondered what I'd do if I had the choice of taking my glory now and having it over by thirty, or being what I am now in order to have a dazzling life later.

I didn't even try to imagine Mike Harbinger being less than terrific at thirty. That was unthinkable.

Meanwhile, there was the other immediate, burning issue. "Out of it is one thing. But not a wimp. Never. Not Bruce Springsteen."

I woke at dawn on Thursday. My father was out trimming hedges and cutting what grass our dogs had spared. Before he left for work, he called Shirley Miller and broke their date for that night, which was sad. He wouldn't be seeing her all weekend, since he was leaving for the mental health convention Friday.

While Shirley was probably not in her glory days, I thought I wouldn't mind being like her when I grow up.

That was the trouble with Shirley. I not only liked and admired her, I couldn't help thinking, in spite of myself, about how it might be if my father married her.

He could hardly expect her to share his Hide-A-Bed sofa in the parlor. Nor could they move into one of the bedrooms and shift Mrs. Farisee or the twins and me to the parlor. The pantry was too small to sleep three kids, and Mrs. Farisee would never consent to being moved in there.

If my father married Shirley, Mrs. Farisee would have to go. Shirley would never object to dogs in the house—she always wrestled around with ours when she came over. Shirley would not only let you go to a Saturday matinee before you cleaned your room, she'd probably come with you.

At the same time, I felt creepy thinking of an-

21

other woman, even Shirley, moving into our house and into the center of my father's life. Worse, I was ashamed that such thoughts could sneak into my mind when I already had a mother.

The most awful thought was that my mother might decide she wanted to come back, after my father had married Shirley.

He did not try to push Mrs. Farisee to do more than her usual work. Instead, he switched around his afternoon appointments so that he was home by the time we got in from school.

The man had no qualms about pushing his own children. He set the twins to washing the bottoms of the windows while I cleaned the tops.

The floors filled him with despair, a despair which Mrs. Farisee felt duty bound to deepen.

"Wax," she declared, "will never restore the surface."

"They didn't look so great when we moved in," I reminded my father.

"And months of dog claws and tracked-in dirt have done them no good." Mrs. Farisee was speaking of the days when she had not been around. Not even the Mongol hordes would track dirt into a house where she ruled. "You'll have to refinish them."

My father rushed out to rent a machine that stripped and waxed floors.

Mrs. Farisee went to a movie so she wouldn't be present for the operation.

My father sent the twins and me out into the yard with the dogs, warning us to keep moving so we wouldn't get chilled. Then he moved furniture, stripped the parts of the floor that showed, and put down a Varathane finish.

He took the twins and me with him to return the machine, and to a drive-in for dinner. By that time he was too exhausted to muster even a roar when Aida, reaching over his shoulder to appropriate the last of his French fries, spilled vanilla milkshake down his neck.

The next morning he overslept, and rushed to work without eating.

"The man is a wreck already," I told Sherman as we walked to school, "and your uncle hasn't even set foot in the house."

My father came home from work with just enough time to throw his things into a suitcase. Mrs. Farisee drove him to the airport. She didn't let us come. "Your father," she said, "is not up to a car full of children."

Left home with strict orders to keep the twins in, the dogs out, the doors locked, and the house neat, I turned on the television in the parlor. Watching my father's set instead of wrangling with the twins over programs was a luxury. Then I got to thinking about all the families in town who had cable.

I found a spy movie set in the Caribbean. While the hero and a beautiful mysterious woman were being stalked through streets clogged with conga dancers and steel-drum bands, our telephone rang. I brought it into the parlor.

It was Sherman. "They're talking condos," he announced.

"Combos?" I kept my eyes on the television screen.

"Condos. My father was just on the phone to Bramwell. The deal is, my dad's pushing the City Council to rezone your neighborhood."

I turned down the set. From the bedroom, I heard the continuing beat of the steel-drum band. I knew I shouldn't let the twins watch a movie that might turn violent, but I had more serious worries.

"Right now, they can only build single-family houses on your block." Sherman's voice was low, like that of somebody calling the police from a public telephone. "See, he plans to sell the houses he owns on your block to my uncle, then get the planning commission to condemn the block, so my uncle can tear down the houses and build condominiums. It won't look good if my father owns all the houses and pushes through the rezoning while he's on the City Council, and then builds the condos. It will look even worse if he gets elected mayor next fall. I'm not sure it would be legal."

I heard the twins opening and closing cupboard doors, but I couldn't even yell at them not to make a mess. Sherman's news had hit me like a poison-tipped blow dart.

He went on in that same guarded voice. "No condo in the world is going to take a family with

24

three dogs, let alone three the size of Herb and Joe and Sadie. From what I gather, my dad expects no trouble in getting the properties condemned, since the city is all gung ho for redevelopment. The eviction process, though, may take a while, especially if Mr. Troup refuses to sell or go quietly. He'll have the time of his life holding everything up."

"Sherman, what are we going to do?"

He was quiet for a long time. Then he murmured, "I don't know, Dez."

We went on talking for a while, but he came up with nothing hopeful. Since his parents had just gone out and their maid was watching television, he didn't really have to worry about being overheard.

When I heard a distinctive engine rattle outside, I hung up and turned off the spy movie and brushed hair and cracker crumbs off the Hide-A-Bed sofa and shooed the dogs into the backyard. Then I went back to our bedroom to be sure the twins hadn't done anything to get me in trouble.

They were making their own steel-drum band out of some empty cans. "Be sure there aren't any sharp edges," I warned.

Mrs. Farisee stuck her head in our bedroom door, said, "I'm back and stop that banging," and went to the kitchen to start dinner.

I helped her. I didn't tell her what Sherman had said. Knowing how she focused on the worst, I was sure she'd have me convinced we'd all be out on the street by Christmas.

After dinner, the twins and I washed dishes, and

25

then Mrs. Farisee set me to my homework even though it was Friday night.

After I finished, I washed my hair. Mrs. Farisee always said that going to bed with a wet head would bring on pneumonia. I figured, what did I have to lose? Even Harley Grove and his brother Bramwell would hesitate to evict a family with a kid recovering from pneumonia, if that kid had once been in the paper for rescuing the landlord's own flesh and blood.

I poured about a quarter-cup from the shampoo bottle over my head, thinking that maybe in the morning I'd go buy a magazine that had hairstyles in it.

It would be neat, I thought, to have a friend to try out hairdos with. We might even admit to each other that we wanted to look older because of Mike Harbinger. We might even share daydreams about him.

It took a minute for me to realize that I had a serious problem. My hair was sticking to my hands. I tried rinsing my hair, but that seemed to make it gummy. Then it started to get stiff.

Mrs. Farisee banged on the bathroom door and told me to stop wasting hot water. I wrapped a towel around my head, and actually went to her for help.

It was a struggle pulling the towel off and even then some of the fuzz stuck to my hair.

While I tried to drag a comb through the tangles,

Mrs. Farisee went to the bathroom and came back with the shampoo bottle. "I threw this in the waste-basket empty this morning. Where did you get it?"

"It was by the sink. Mrs. Farisee, the comb is caught in my hair."

It took two of us to free the comb, and then I was barely able to get my hands off my head.

Mrs. Farisee strode into the bedroom, where the twins were watching "Friday Night Chillers" with the sound off. She turned off the picture and interrogated them.

Since they had no idea they'd done anything wrong, they freely admitted that they'd used the polyurethane tin for their steel-drum band. They had even saved the last of the stuff by pouring it into the empty shampoo bottle, which they had left by the sink.

They were fascinated by the results, watching silently as Mrs. Farisee and I tried everything from vinegar to salad oil on my hair as the Varathane hardened.

She even turned up the water heater so I could try to shampoo with regular hand soap.

Finally, she said I'd have to use her hair dryer before exhaustion guaranteed me pneumonia. When I finished using the dryer, she came into the bathroom with a green-and-orange paisley print scarf of hers. "Here. Tie up your head so you don't catch a draft. We'll think of something in the morning."

three

In the morning, all she could think of was professional help.

Sherman had come over early, as he usually did.

"Oh, wow, Dez," he breathed, gazing at my hair. Instead of lying flat, it stood up in clumps and spikes, probably because I'd spent a restless night.

Sherman, of course, had known me from the time my hair had just started coming back. After my mother left, my hair had fallen out until I had a little bald spot on top. The psychologist my father sent me to said it was from stress, and in time my hair did grow in. I suppose Sherman felt it was especially poignant that it had returned only to be Varathaned.

"There has got to be something made that will dissolve this guck," I said, trying hard not to cry.

"Varnish remover," Mrs. Farisee said, "and it would peel the scalp right off you."

"You try any more stuff on your head, Dez,"

Sherman agreed, "and you might get some really weird chemical reaction."

The twins edged closer, obviously hoping that I might bring about a reaction so spectacular it would make their Saturday.

"Of course, I don't know any beauty shop that will take you without an appointment on a weekend." Mrs. Farisee always felt obliged to mention the worst possible outcome.

I got out the telephone book anyway, and leafed through the yellow pages, half afraid Mrs. Farisee might offer to take me to the beauty shop she used. Her hair lay in still, perfect curls, like a colony of ghostly lavender-tinted snail shells.

Sherman, looking over my shoulder, put his finger on the Mona Lisa Salon ad. "That's in the Rancho Grande Mall. My uncle Bramwell owns the whole mall."

"Tell them," Mrs. Farisee suggested. "You might get a discount."

I telephoned the Mona Lisa and explained that it was an emergency, but I couldn't bring myself to mention Bramwell Grove.

After all, it was partly due to him and his condo plans that my head was polyurethaned.

I got an appointment for ten o'clock.

Mrs. Farisee said I could not go to a beauty shop wearing jeans, so I went to the bedroom to change. The twins took their ant farm into the kitchen to show Sherman.

My mother had sent it to them for their birthday.

My mother had always had a feeling for animals. She had rescued more than I could count, pulling off the freeway to help some crazed lanky hound out of the traffic, squatting in the rain in a downtown parking lot to coax a half-wild, terrified cat to her.

Then she left us—to find herself, she explained.

When she left, she was a person who would not have a mousetrap in the house. Whoever she had found had given her own kids a bunch of ants sealed in plastic.

I didn't want to think about what had happened to her, but I couldn't stop. Either she had changed, or she had sold out to be like everybody else, or she was so busy she remembered the birthday at the last minute and just bought anything without considering. To buy an ant farm, though, meant she had changed.

There was the other possibility. Maybe she hadn't taken time to buy it herself, but had asked somebody to pick out a present for her kids. Maybe some boyfriend had selected it and even mailed it for her.

Thinking about her and that ant farm hurt so much I hoped she'd just forget my birthday.

Antony and Aida watched the ant farm sometimes, maybe because it was a present from their mother, but you can't get thrilled about a bunch of trapped ants.

I felt under the bunk bed for my left shoe. How

can you clean your room and still lose a shoe? I wondered. I rummaged through the wastebasket and dresser drawers, until the room began to look as it had before we cleaned it.

While I was standing on a chair feeling over the closet shelf, I heard Sherman worrying aloud about how the ants must feel spending their lives in a plastic prison.

Nobody else had had the heart to tell the twins what a monstrous thing the farm was.

Before he could upset Antony and Aida too much, I yelled, "Sherman! Look in the parlor and see if my shoe is under anything."

I began tossing stuff out of the twins' toy box, even though I knew I'd have to put it all back. As I hauled out dirty socks, crumpled paper, gum wrappers, and parts of toys, I heard Antony in the kitchen.

"Wait. Wait. Wait," he said urgently. "You can't just turn them loose without anything to eat."

Right away, I knew what was going on.

I hurried into the kitchen with my right shoe untied. Antony was taking a jar of honey from the refrigerator. Aida stood holding the farm and weeping quietly, I suppose at the prospect of parting with the ants.

"Would a chewed-up thong do?" Sherman yelled from the parlor.

"You've got to take it well away from the house," I told the twins, "and then pry it open without hurting them. They'll need just a spoonful of

31

honey." I went out to the back porch and looked for a screwdriver.

There was a wail from the kitchen, and a crash. I ran back in time to see Antony run to the fridge and stick his wet, scalded hand into the freezer compartment.

Hot water was still running over the broken honey jar in the sink. A few ants were beginning to leak out of the farm Aida had dropped when Antony scalded his hand.

"What is going on in here?" Mrs. Farisee came rushing in from her room.

I started to explain that Antony had been trying to soften the honey by running hot water over the jar, when he let out another yowl. By then, of course, his hand was stuck firmly to the freezer wall.

While Herb and Joe and Sadie scratched at the back door and howled to come in, Mrs. Farisee disconnected the refrigerator and we poured warm water over my brother's hand to thaw him loose. Sherman and Aida looked on, awed and silent.

The scalded part of Antony's hand was red and puffy, with dead white frostbite in the center. Mrs. Farisee carried him out to my father's car while I ran after her with her purse. "Remember your hair appointment," she told me as she belted Antony in. *"And get rid of those ants!"*

I herded my sister back into the house, Sherman following.

As we squatted in the kitchen, watching the ants spill out of the cracked farm, Sherman said, "Boy.

32

Not many kids his age can scald and freeze themselves at the same time."

"It's not easy to run hot water over something you're holding without running hot water over your hand," I pointed out. "And I used so much on my hair last night that Mrs. Farisee turned up the water heater."

"How are we going to catch the ants without hurting them?" Aida asked.

"There's got to be a way," I said.

"Bags!" Sherman said. "Plastic bags!"

Since it was his idea, I made him pick up the ant farm while I held the plastic trash bag. Being, as my father had noted, a gentle soul, Sherman couldn't wash off the ants that swarmed up his fingers. With Aida trailing him anxiously, he ran outside and tried to shake free of them. While Aida begged him not to hurt the ants, the dogs barked and jumped on him delightedly.

By the time Sherman and my sister came in, I'd put a second and third bag over the first, securing each tightly.

"How are they going to breathe?" Aida was already pale and teary from Antony's ordeal.

"There is enough air in there for ants," I assured her. "Trust me. Believe me."

"What about the ants loose in the kitchen?"

"First, we've got to do something with the whole farm. Then we'll come back and find a good home for the stragglers."

"What about the broken jar?"

"Aida, ants are too small to get cut on glass. They are too small to swallow glass. This has been scientifically proven."

I went back to our room to look for my shoe. Whatever happened, I could not be late to the Mona Lisa. You don't wrangle a Saturday appointment by pleading emergency and then arrive late. Not only would I be turned away, the receptionist might not be able to work me in for days. Meanwhile, moment by moment, polyurethane might be penetrating my scalp and destroying my brain.

To get to the Mona Lisa, I had to go out in public. Baring my hair was unthinkable. I looked around for the scarf Mrs. Farisee had loaned me. I ransacked the room again.

Then I had a moment's good sense. I pulled down my bedspread. The scarf was still on my pillow.

I looked under the pillow for my shoe, but that was expecting too much. Taking off my right shoe, I padded out to the back porch and put on my rain boots. These were not fashion boots. These were strictly for storms, so clunky you would never want to be seen on the street in them unless the skies had already opened.

But no one would be looking at my feet.

For all her tender feelings, my sister has a practical streak. She had ferreted out half a dozen soda bottles and put them in the wagon with the ant bags. "I'll trade them in to buy comic books," she explained.

"You want me to come with you?" Sherman asked me.

"You? *You?*" Then I saw how anxious and miserable he looked. There was no point in reminding him that but for his relatives, but for his own talk of stir-crazy ants, none of these catastrophes would have happened. Once I got started, I might get so carried away I'd make myself late to the Mona Lisa. "I think you'd better go home," I told him, as calmly as I could.

He plugged in the refrigerator and left.

So, at twelve and a half, an age when merely being seen in the wrong cut of jeans can ruin you socially, I had to walk all the way to the Rancho Grande Mall looking like a refugee from a Latvian potato farm, with my little sister pulling a wagon full of ants and bottles.

At her best, Aida resembled a bag lady in training. Mrs. Farisee, in her early weeks as our housekeeper, had been determined to keep Aida presentable. This was like trying to hold back a glacier. Slowly, inexorably, from the time she bathed and combed and dressed herself in the morning, my sister began accumulating skinned knees, rips, and tangles in a general decline toward total grubbiness.

The Rancho Grande Mall was a rundown shopping center a dozen blocks from our house, in a neighborhood of service stations and World War Two tract houses, with no place where we could leave an ant colony without being noticed.

Between a coin-operated laundry and a shoe-repair shop was a wide display window with *Mona Lisa Salon de Beauté* swirled in pink script across it, and a glass door with a sign that read *Open Evenings, Appointments Not Necessary.*

"You'll have to leave the wagon outside," I told my sister.

"I'll stay here with it," she said.

I don't know whether she was worried that some wagon-napper might swoop by, or whether she wanted to be with the ants as long as possible, but I was relieved.

"Then you stay right by the window," I told her sternly. "You do not move an inch, and you do not speak to a soul."

She nodded.

I knew she would obey my orders to the letter. After the morning we'd had, she wouldn't dare provoke me.

I slunk into the Mona Lisa Salon.

A stocky woman with blue eye shadow sat at the front desk reading *Soap Opera Digest.* Her hair looked like the spun glass that fancy department stores use for clouds in Christmas displays.

"My name is Desdemona Blank," I said. "I have an appointment with Miss Lisa."

Flicking me with a quick glance, she dismissed me as nobody to respect. She put down the magazine and stood, pulling down the skirt of her shiny pink nylon uniform. "Okay. Come on."

To establish some kind of relationship, I added, "I'm a friend of Bramwell Grove's nephew."

The woman sat down again. "Mona!" she yelled. "You take this one."

"I think the appointment was with Miss Lisa," I reminded her, thinking she had been absorbed in her reading when I first said it.

"I'm going to be booked up."

A woman in an almost identical pink uniform and hair like cotton candy came from behind a curtain at the rear of the shop, advancing with heavy step and narrowed eyes. "Whataya mean, take this one? Isn't this your ten o'clock?"

"You take this one and I'll close up tonight."

Mona gazed at me with all the cheer of somebody reading a midwinter utility bill.

"I wonder if you could put me kind of near the back, but where I could still see out the window," I ventured.

Mona steered me to the closest chair. "Take off the kerchief."

I didn't want to lose both Mona and Lisa with my hair still varnished, so I sat down and untied the scarf.

"Wha . . . she's shellacked!" Mona cried. "Lisa, look at this!"

Lisa sidled around the desk and, standing beside Mona, gingerly poked my hair with an enameled fingernail. "It's solid."

Mona was stern. "Kid, this may seem like a ter-

rific new fad to you, but, believe me, you're wreck-
ing your hair varnishing it."

"I didn't. My brother and sister—"

"They *varnished* you?" Mona demanded.

Turning her head away from me slightly, Lisa
muttered to Mona, "Friends of Bram Grove."

"My father refinished the floors," I explained.
"When my brother and sister used the varnish tin
to make a drum, they emptied the Varathane into a
shampoo bottle and left it in the bathroom."

Mona and Lisa asked no more questions, but con-
ferred about the remedy for my condition. Everything Mona suggested, Lisa vetoed. Everything Lisa
came up with, Mona rejected. Aida kept glancing in,
troubled by their growing vehemence.

"We got to go trial and error here," Mona declared finally, and finally Lisa agreed.

They sprayed my hair with hot water. It ran off
my head like rain from a tile roof. They tried to
massage in shampoo and gel and creme and mousse,
but my hair remained solid and impervious.

Mona and Lisa got sweaty and flushed and more
snappish. Every few minutes, Aida peered in, but
the atmosphere was so tense she didn't dare step
inside.

Finally Mona and Lisa became calm, like death-
row cellmates who realize they're stuck with each
other. Withdrawing to the rear of the shop, they
caucused urgently, whispering at each other more
and more vehemently.

When they came back, they looked at me in the

mirror, and then Mona said, "Honey, there's no way around it. The hair has got to go."

With the two of them agreeing, I knew they had to be right.

I wanted desperately to grab the scarf and run out of there, but I knew my father and Mrs. Farisee would never let me walk around with floor finish on my head.

Mona and Lisa began wrangling even more hotly over the *way* to cut my hair. Finally, Mona went across the mall to the television repair shop and borrowed a couple of screwdrivers. She used them like chopsticks, working them through my hair to pry a chunk free and hold it up while Lisa cut it off.

Closing my eyes, I forced myself to sit without a whimper, without a shudder, as each lock struck my shoulders or clunked on the floor. I knew that any movement might destroy Lisa's concentration.

At last she said, "If we cut any more you'll look like a loofah. Tell your mother—"

"My mother's . . . away." I opened my eyes, but I was careful not to look at a mirror.

"Tell your father that when it grows out you'll look—"

"Better," Mona said.

"Somewhat," Lisa added. "Tell him we did the best we could and there's no sense him coming in here making a scene."

"He won't. He's traveling."

I tied on the scarf, unable to look at Mona and Lisa.

I was at the desk, counting out money for Mona, when I heard Sherman's voice outside. "Hey, Aida. Dez in there?"

Sherman entered with a man who sauntered in like a movie star arriving for a press conference. Tall, with thick, glossy black hair and dark eyes, he was handsome in a tense way, faintly menacing like the heroes on the covers of the paperback romances Mrs. Farisee bought at the supermarket. He wore a black, double-breasted cashmere overcoat, black gloves, dark trousers, a silky scarf, and supple black shoes.

"I got a ride with my uncle," Sherman greeted me.

It is not easy to discourage a wimp who is devoted to you.

Sherman's uncle ignored me. "So, Lisa, how's it going?"

"Business is terrible and I'm Mona." Her voice was flat and wary.

"Whatever. The rent check you told me was in the mail last week never came."

"We didn't count on your hiking the rent twice in a year," Lisa told him.

"Everybody's got to live, ladies. I can't support the world."

"We haven't cleared three hundred this week," Mona said.

"I'll take it now, cash, the balance next week."

When adults are talking like this, the best thing

to do is pretend you don't understand. I studied the pictures of hairstyles on the walls.

Mona and Lisa collected cash from the register and their handbags and Bramwell took it and said he'd return in a week. Aiming a pat at Sherman's head, he told him, "See ya, kid," and strode from the salon.

Mona took my money and counted out my change in dimes and quarters. "So your father's a traveling salesman and your uncle's—"

"No, no," I corrected her hastily. "That's *Sherman's* uncle."

"Try to take after the other side of your family," Mona advised him.

Aida stuck her head in the door. "Can we do something about my ants now?"

"If your aunts are related to Bram Grove, don't recommend this place to them," Lisa told me.

Sherman followed me from the salon. "So let's see how they fixed your hair."

"It looked as if they were cutting it to the *skin,*" Aida said.

"Take her to trade in the bottles," I told Sherman.

Aida hauled the wagon across the street to the market, talking steadily to Sherman. I sat on the edge of a concrete planter box, under a stunted, leafless tree. Feeling the cold wind through my scarf, I put my head down so that nobody would notice if I started to cry.

Sherman and Aida were gone so long I knew she was either reading all the comics on the racks or stalled over which to buy.

While I was deciding whether to go get her, she came out of the supermarket with Sherman and crossed the parking lot, pulling the wagon and shaking carob chips out of a bag into her mouth. I knew she'd bought them because they were cheap, being sold in bulk. It was too late to wonder how many other kids had had their hands in the bin.

"Watch out for cars, dummy!" I yelled.

There I was, sitting on a planter box with my head tied up in a kerchief, which probably did not hide the fact that I was nearly bald. I was yelling in a voice like an elephant seal's at my sister, who was pulling a wagon full of ant farm and shaking carob chips into her face while crossing a parking lot. With her was our landlord's eleven-year-old wimp son, my best friend in the world.

And there were Mike Harbinger and his friends, not twenty feet away, looking at me.

The wind whipped a hamburger wrapper across the lot and tugged at the back point of my scarf.

Holding down the kerchief, I dashed over to grab Aida and hurry away from Mike Harbinger.

"What about my ants?" Aida kept asking me. "What about the ants?"

"You can't bring them home, Dez," Sherman warned.

We were at the very margin of the mall before I stopped. On our left was a raised rectangular island

42

landscaped with rocks and juniper. I nodded toward it. "They've got to live outside, Aida, or somebody is sure to spray them or stomp them."

Shoving the chips into her coat pocket, Aida climbed up on the planter, clutching the trash bags.

"Hey." Bramwell Grove came out the back door of the bakery. "What are you dumping in there?"

Sherman was too taken aback to start with a good explanation and then work up gradually to the answer. "Ants."

Bramwell Grove was more formidable than most adults. Instead of looking blank, or surprised, he exploded instantly. "Ants? Live ants? You're putting live ants in my mall?"

"Harmless ants," I said hastily. "My sister's ant farm is cracked and they're kind of leaking out."

"You don't have a trash can at home?" Bramwell asked coldly.

"We're trying to find the ants a warm, safe place to live," Sherman explained.

Bramwell put a hand on his nephew's shoulder. "Kid, there is no such place."

My sister stood, scared and uncertain, looking up at Bramwell. Aida is not cute, or pert, or cuddly. What Aida is, is sincere.

Bramwell Grove looked down at her. Aida looked up at him. His gaze shifted. Then, sounding exasperated and embarrassed, he growled, "Will you hurry it up, then? You want people to see me hanging out with a bunch of kids that relocate ants?"

Hastily, fumbling, as if afraid he might change his

43

mind, Aida undid the twist-ties and shook out the plastic bags. Ants crawled onto her like shipwreck survivors onto an island.

I had not realized just how many ants that farm contained.

As she brushed and shook herself, I stood for a second, too astonished to realize she needed rescuing.

Bramwell Grove gazed at the spectacle. "You ever see that Charlton Heston movie where he's in the jungle and millions of army ants go on the march?"

"Yeah," Sherman said. "Like, they strip an elephant to the bones in—"

"For Pete's sake!" Shoving me aside, a woman set her grocery bags on the ledge and leaped onto the island. Even as I recognized Shirley Miller, Sherman jumped up to help her.

The three of us picked ants off Aida, then shook them off our arms, shoes, fingers. Finally Shirley lifted Aida off the island and brushed a few more ants from her coat.

"I don't even want to know why," Shirley said.

It was typical of Shirley that she didn't ask how we came to be dumping ants from a plastic bag into a shopping center. She would assume we had a legitimate reason. "Where's your brother?"

"He froze his hand and Mrs. Farisee rushed him to the hospital," I said.

"First he scalded it under hot water, then he put it in the refrigerator and it stuck to the freezer

44

part." Though I'm certain Sherman would have proposed to Shirley if he'd been sixteen, he was far from dumbstruck in her presence.

She shook her head in sympathy, then looked up at the sky. "You'd better get home before the storm hits. I'd drive you, but my car's in the shop."

Bramwell Grove regarded her with a mixture of respect and interest, like an explorer who has come upon a puzzling but highly advanced civilization. Even in an old raincoat, she looked lean and lithe, and definitely not his type. "Could I give you a lift?" he asked her.

"My uncle Bramwell," Sherman admitted grudgingly.

"Great," Shirley told Bramwell. "I wouldn't want the kids to get caught in the rain—and if these grocery bags get soaked before I make it home, I'm going to be leaving a trail of canned cat food."

She hoisted one of the bags, and as she bent to pick up the other, he lifted it, but he didn't try to relieve her of the one she already had. Smart, I thought. He's already sizing her up. That made me uneasy.

Shirley took Aida's hand, Aida took the wagon handle, and we followed Bramwell to a new, dark blue, long, low car, like something Ricardo Montalban would advertise on television. As Bramwell glanced at Aida's wagon, I was very sure that if Shirley had not been with us, he would never have allowed that wagon near that car.

He rested the bag on the rear bumper, and unlocked the trunk. "Clean off the wagon," he told my sister.

Aida gave the rear wheels a swipe with her coat sleeve.

Meanwhile, I was worrying about whether to accept the ride or get caught in the rain. Sherman, my closest friend, was coming with us, as was Shirley, my father's girlfriend.

This was Sherman's uncle, who owned the mall and might soon own our house.

I was pretty sure all this didn't add up to justification for taking a ride from the man.

As he unlocked the trunk, I edged closer to Shirley and whispered, "Can you ask him to take us home first?"

"Absolutely," she murmured.

Bramwell put the groceries, then the wagon, in the trunk.

Shirley sat in the front with him.

The upholstery in the car was midnight blue crushed velvet, and the dashboard and door panels were inlaid wood. Besides an instrument panel that must have taken weeks to learn, there was a telephone and a sound system. Before he started the engine, Bramwell inserted a cassette into the player on the dash, and then turned the quadraphonic sound down low.

"I've got to pick up some ledgers first," he told Shirley. "Sorry if it's out of your way, but I need them for my next stop."

He drove downtown, through its core to its husk, to streets with karate studios and resale clothing stores, then streets with surplus stores and boarded-over buildings, pawnshops and bail-bond establishments, and finally streets of movie houses with posters he ordered us not to look at.

I knew I would never, whatever the circumstances, take another ride with anybody without getting permission from Mrs. Farisee or my father. I'd been uncertain when I thought Bramwell was taking us right home—and here we were riding through this awful part of town.

"This is a scary neighborhood," Sherman observed.

"Are you kidding? It's a gold mine," his uncle told him.

"This?" Sherman asked.

Bramwell turned the music down even more. "The whole area's condemned. Town's going to tear everything down and build an industrial park. And I own half the buildings. That, kid, is known as foresight."

Though he was addressing Sherman, he seemed to be talking more to Shirley.

On the next street all the structures looked abandoned. Bramwell parked in front of a three-story building. Though slogans had been spray-painted on every wall around it, it stood unmarked.

Bramwell got out. "Back in a second," he told Shirley. "Keep the doors and windows locked."

Shirley gazed after him as he entered the building. "Interesting personality."

"My mother calls him a slumlord," Sherman confided. "She gets all upset when Mr. Troup calls my father that, but I guess in my uncle's case she thinks it fits."

The sidewalks were littered, and the only living creature I saw was a lank and ribby dog that shambled out of the alley. His coat was sparse and patchy, his muzzle grizzled. His gait was unsteady, as if he were trying not to lie down and give up. He had, overall, the look of a dog with a history that would break your heart.

"Find the button that opens the trunk, Dez, and lock the door after me." Ignoring Bramwell's advice, Shirley got out of the car.

As she approached the dog, he crouched to protect his hindquarters and lifted one placating paw, as if to apologize for his existence.

Scrambling into the front seat, I examined the dashboard, trying to decide what would lock the door and open the trunk.

Shirley reached for the dog. He cringed, trembling, but she edged closer, talking all the time, until she touched his head.

Bramwell came out of the building carrying several black ledgers.

"Slow down," Shirley told him quietly. "Open the trunk and see what I've got to feed him. Give me the frozen fruit bars, too. He's probably thirsty."

It's just what my mother would have done, I thought, *at least before the ant farm.*

"This is not a neighborhood to hang around in," Bramwell told Shirley.

"I know," she said. "Not fit for a dog."

He unlocked the trunk and, moving carefully, brought her a box of fruit bars and another of crackers.

She was right. As she broke the bars off their sticks, the dog gulped them desperately. While he ate the crackers with the same urgency, he was too gentle to snap them out of her hands.

Bramwell stood watching her. "Better get going."

She looked up. "Could you keep him overnight while I figure out what to do with him?"

"*Do* with him?"

"You can see he's starving. We'll have to take him—"

"Not in my car."

Shirley stood. "May I use your car phone to call a cab?"

"You think a cabbie's going to come down here for a fare, even if he'd take you with that mutt?"

She walked around to the passenger door. "Dez, you call home and explain that Sherman and his uncle are driving you. Take my groceries into your house, and I'll be there as soon as I can." She walked back to the dog, who had not taken his eyes off her. "Let's go," she told him.

They'd gone only a few steps when Bramwell

strode after them. "You know you can't be out on these streets alone."

She kept going, the dog at her side.

Sherman scrambled into the driver's seat and out of the car. Before I could stop her, Aida followed.

This was not an area in which you yelled, or called attention to yourself in any way. Instead of ordering my sister back, I went after her.

"I'm talking to you!" Bramwell caught up with Shirley. "You think that fleabag is any protection in a neighborhood like this?"

"Maybe you'll be kind enough to call the police if I get in trouble—provided you think they'll come down here."

Bramwell stepped in front of her. "You're trying to make me look like some kind of . . ." He hauled Sherman around beside him. "Would I hurt a dog? Tell her."

"Not unless it owed you money."

Bramwell looked down at his nephew appraisingly. "You got your mother's mouth on you, kid."

"I'm not leaving this animal out on the street," Shirley said. "Look at him. You can see every bone in his body."

It was too much for my sister. Squatting beside the dog, she threw her arms around his neck and began crying quietly.

The dog licked her ear.

If there is a man who can stand up to a righteous woman, a starving dog, and a weeping child, I don't want to meet him.

50

Bramwell looked around the deserted streets as if to challenge anyone watching us. He glanced down at my sister sniffling against the dog's snout. He glared at me, then at Sherman, who shrugged.

"Get in the car, will you?" he growled. "And keep that hound in your lap in case he's not upholstery-broken," he told Shirley.

"Let me hold him," Sherman pleaded. Sherman had a dog of sorts, six pounds of macho canine swagger. Whenever Sherman brought him to our house, Jake was always snarling and insulting Herb and Joe when he wasn't sidling up to Sadie. Being ten or twelve times his size, our three strove to ignore him. They seemed vaguely embarrassed by Jake, as if he might be mistaken for one of their species. I could see how Sherman would be captivated by this mild, sweet-tempered, down-and-out animal.

As we got in the car, Shirley lifted the dog and put him in Sherman's lap. "When you get home, you'd better wash your clothes and take a shower right away."

Bramwell started the engine. "Should I shower my upholstery or just rip it out?"

"Spray it," she said calmly.

Bramwell drove on silently, not even turning on his quadraphonic music. Sherman stroked the dog's head.

Bramwell glanced at them in the rearview mirror. "That mutt's no spring chicken, you know."

Sherman held the dog closer.

"Don't get me wrong," Bramwell went on before Shirley could speak. "I got nothing against dogs. When I was little, I wanted one, just like any kid. I was always after my parents to get one, but they wouldn't, because of Harley."

"My father didn't like dogs?" Sherman asked.

"I don't know about like," his uncle said. "He was scared to death of them—froze if so much as a chihuahua came sniffing around him."

That, I thought, explained why Sherman never got a dog when he was little, and why the one his parents finally got him was so tiny.

"It's true what they say, you know," Bramwell added darkly. "Dogs can scent fear. I swear they can. Anyplace we went, they were always after Harley, nosing at his heels, trying to shake hands, all those dumb dog tricks, trying to make up with him. Me, somehow I never had a way with dogs. I always pictured myself with one, maybe a Doberman or a pit bull. But dogs just never seemed to take to me. You know how many times I've been bit trying to pet one? Or they wait until I turn my back and then fang me in the ankle."

"That's sad." Aida's sympathies, which were active to begin with, were getting a heavy workout this day.

"Did you ever have a pet?" Sherman asked.

"I raised Siamese fighting fish for a while. There used to be a lot of money in fighting fish. Now there's a glut on the market. I still think one of

these days I might find a dog I can get along with."
He slid a new cassette into the player on the dashboard.

At the first notes, the stray on Sherman's lap
began to howl.

Bramwell turned off the player. "Where do you
live?" he asked me.

I told him our address, not reminding him that he
might be buying the place.

He didn't even ask Shirley her address, though,
for all he knew, she lived closer.

As we reached our street, Sherman said, "It's a
crummy block, but it would be a shame to change
it. There aren't that many people around able to
pay higher rents."

"People will pay what they have to," Bramwell
said.

"Is your basement still damp?" Sherman asked
me. "That's probably because your house is built on
fill land. This whole block is probably soggy, if you
dig deep enough. It was probably a mistake to build
anything here in the first place."

Sherman has some great qualities.

"I don't know what I'm going to do about this animal." Shirley sounded worried. "I live in a one-
room apartment where even my cat is contraband."

I was afraid she'd ask us to keep the dog. If we
were barely hanging on to our house, one more
beast was all the excuse Harley Grove would need
to kick us out. Even if we hid the dog when he and

Bramwell came to see the house, Bramwell would know, and when it came to business, I suspected Harley Grove was a softie next to Bramwell.

Shirley, of course, knew better than to ask any renters with three animals to take in a fourth, at least not while the landlord's brother was listening. Also, she had met Mrs. Farisee. "Sherman, do you think—"

"Jake would tear right into him. Besides, it took me most of my life to get Jake."

"Tell Antony I hope his hand's okay," Shirley said, as Aida and I got out of the car. "I'd come in, but . . ."

"But that would be holding me up even more," Bramwell said, locking the car door after us.

As Aida and I reached the porch, the rain started.

four

Mrs. Farisee was sitting on the sofa. My brother was beside her sipping hot chocolate from one of our good cups while she held the saucer for him.

She had never before let any of us eat or drink in the parlor.

Antony looked tired and pale. His right hand was bandaged all the way up the wrist. Even Mrs. Farisee looked worn out. While a hurricane could never muss those lavender curls, her blue eyes looked pale and watery and bloodshot.

What surprised me was that my brother was sitting so close to her. She had always seemed to me like a combination housekeeper and warden. Still, in the first hours after my hair was varnished, she'd been my only resource.

"There's some soup and more hot chocolate on the stove," she told us. "The rest of your lunch is in the fridge."

It was the first time she'd ever been so slapdash about meals.

What with relocating the ants and observing Bramwell and meeting Shirley and rescuing the dog, I'd almost forgotten that I was clipped like a Marine recruit. Being in the house with a kerchief on reminded me now, but I didn't take it off. I wasn't ready to face even the reactions of Mrs. Farisee and my own brother.

I poured soup and hot chocolate for myself and Aida, reminding her, as I always did, that there was no need to add sugar to hot chocolate. From the refrigerator, I took our sandwiches, neatly made and wrapped in plastic.

We didn't presume to bring our lunches into the parlor, knowing that if Antony hadn't required emergency medical care, he wouldn't be drinking in there either.

Thinking of my hair had all but destroyed my appetite. After we finished our chocolate and soup, I put my sandwich back in the refrigerator.

We tidied the kitchen and went in to see how our brother was.

The rain had stopped, and through the front window I saw a car pull up at the curb. It was new, and elegant, though not in a class with Bramwell's. A little boy got out and came to our door. When I opened the door, he turned and waved to the driver, and the car pulled away. Turning back to me, he handed me his furled umbrella and began unbuttoning his trench coat. "I'm Preston." He gave no last name, as if "Preston" were all the world needed to know.

It was plain this kid was not selling mints or tickets to a raffle. I felt as if I were caught in the opening of a television series. Had we won him? Had he adopted us? Could he be the child of some millionaire fifth cousins we'd never met, a rich waif who'd run away from home and come to us for shelter?

Preston was not put off by my bewilderment. Balancing with one hand on the doorjamb, he took off his right rain boot, then his left. "Where's Antony?"

"Antony?" I was dumbfounded. Nobody had ever come to visit my brother.

Antony wasn't tall for a five-year-old, but this boy was even shorter. Still, his air of confidence was unsettling. He had dark eyes, a round face, and thick, straight, dark brown hair, impeccably cut.

He even had color-coordinated raingear, not the yellow slicker and red vinyl boots most kindergartners wore. His coat was a camel-color fleece-lined twill. His umbrella and boots were a matched dark brown.

As he lined up his boots on the porch, I turned toward the parlor. "Antony? You know a Preston?"

Antony handed Mrs. Farisee his cup. "Oh, yeah. I forgot. I invited him over."

We knew we were never, never to invite a friend over without permission from Mrs. Farisee. Inasmuch as none of us had gotten to know anybody that well since we came to town, and inasmuch as Mrs. Farisee regarded Sherman as a pest who came with the job, the rule had never been tested.

I suppose Mrs. Farisee figured a scalded frozen hand and a morning at the emergency room excused Antony's forgetting, because she only said, "We don't keep guests standing at the door, Desdemona."

I stepped back and Preston stepped in.

"Wow!" He stared at Antony's bandaged hand. "Wow! What happened?"

"I burned it, then I froze it," Antony told him.

"Wow! How?"

While Antony explained, I took Aida out of the parlor and hung up Preston's coat in the hall closet. My brother seldom said more than ten words in a row to anybody but his sister, and I didn't want to do anything to make him or his guest uncomfortable.

Aida went back to our bedroom and I wandered into the kitchen. Mrs. Farisee had put the teakettle on.

I don't know what it would take to make Preston uncomfortable. I could hear him in the parlor, peppering Antony's narrative with *wow*s. Ten words? My brother was spilling out hundreds.

When Antony finished, Preston said, "You'll probably get in trouble if you get the bandage dirty right away. We'd better play in your room."

As they headed for the bedroom, I heard him ask,

"Why does that girl wear a scarf on her head in the house?"

"Why does she?" Mrs. Farisee asked me.

"Because I don't want to show my hair, even to myself."

"Sooner or later you'll have to." She set out two cups and put a chamomile tea bag in each. "Take it off. You look foolish."

One doesn't say no to Mrs. Farisee. I untied the scarf, folded it, and put it on the table.

She gazed at my head. "Oh." She took her aspirin bottle off the shelf over the stove and shook out a couple of pills, which she set on one of the saucers. "Well."

It would have been easier if she'd laughed.

The kettle shrieked and she poured hot water into the cups, put them on the saucers, and brought them to the table. Sitting down heavily, she slid the sugar bowl toward me.

While I was waiting for my tea to cool, she popped the aspirins into her mouth and washed them down. Even in a time of stress, she did not gulp.

Aida wandered into the kitchen. Having already seen my shearing in process, she barely glanced at my hair.

"Did they kick you out of the bedroom?" I asked her.

Aida shook her head. "They don't care where I go."

Mrs. Farisee did not permit us to eat between

meals, but now she said, "Why don't you take an apple?"

My sister shook her head.

"How come," I heard Preston ask, "you have three beds in one room?"

"Three of us sleep in here," Antony said.

"Three?"

"My sisters and I."

"Wow! I never shared a room with anybody."

"You want to see my butterfly collection?"

"No." Preston was firm. "I think it's really rotten to catch butterflies."

"I don't mean live butterflies. You think I'd go around catching live *butterflies*? That's *gross*."

"I don't want to see a bunch of dead ones, either. That's even grosser."

"I build them," Antony explained.

My brother would never torment or trap or catch or kill a living creature. That was one of the fine things about him. I worried, though. How would a kid as self-possessed as this Preston feel about a boy who constructed butterflies from tissue paper, wire, and watercolors?

"Oh, wow!" This *wow* was the most sincere Preston had yet uttered, and Preston had already struck me as a master of the sincere *wow*. "Wow! They are . . . oh, wow! Hey, did you ever build model airplanes?"

"No," Antony confessed.

"Listen, I got this model airplane kit for my

60

birthday, but my father put it away until I'm old enough not to wreck it. If I could show him one of your butterflies, I bet he'd let us make that plane together."

Sitting at the kitchen table, Aida licked the tip of her finger and picked up sugar grains with it. She didn't even scan the floor for ants to rescue.

After I finished my tea, I went into the bathroom. I shut the door and looked in the mirror.

It was worse than I'd expected. The half-inch reddish-brown stubble on my head stood up like new-mowed grass. My eyes seemed enormous, and my ears looked indecent.

For a minute, I felt like throwing up. Then I sat on the edge of the tub, too desolate to cry.

It would be a long, long time before I walked home by way of the football field again.

I thought about facing school on Monday, but the idea was so inconceivably dreadful, I couldn't imagine how it would be.

I got up. The thing to do was keep moving, keep busy.

I couldn't go into the bedroom and set off another commentary by Preston. I fished a sweatshirt and a pair of jeans out of the clothes hamper, then got my old windbreaker from the hall closet and went back to the kitchen. "I promised Dad I'd finish weeding the backyard," I told Mrs. Farisee. "May I borrow your scarf back?"

"You'd better keep it."

As I tied the scarf on, she said, "Be sure to wear your rain boots, and if it's too raw out, you come back in."

I nodded. *With any luck, the weather will be vile,* I thought, *and I'll come down with something that will keep me out of school a month, and my family quarantined in this house even longer.*

I'd been working a few minutes when Aida came out, bundled up and booted. She pulled weeds steadily, without talking, only glancing up at our bedroom window now and then.

I don't know how long we'd been outside when Mrs. Farisee opened the back door. "Your father's on the phone."

I pulled off my windbreaker and the scarf as Aida and I came in the back door.

Our telephone was on a small, high table in the hall, where it was impossible to carry on a private conversation. The cord was so long and the hall so short, you could take the telephone into the parlor, the bedroom, or the kitchen, where Mrs. Farisee had it now.

Aida didn't even try to talk first. She stood listening to me. Leaving the string beans she was fixing in the colander, Mrs. Farisee went to fetch Antony.

"You heard about the ants and Antony's hand?" I asked my father.

"Oh, yes."

"He has company."

"Antony?"

"Some kid about his age. Must be from school."

"Great! How are they getting along?"

"Fine."

"How's everything else?"

I looked at my sister, who was sitting on a kitchen chair looking out the window. "Okay."

I didn't ask him whether Mrs. Farisee had told him about my hair. I couldn't bear to bring it up. It wasn't likely that she had—a son's frozen scalded hand was enough for a father to hear about long distance. I didn't mention seeing Shirley, either, since there was no point getting into the matter of my taking a ride without permission. "How's the convention?"

"Not bad. Is Mrs. Farisee still taking you all to the museum tonight?"

"Unless it would be better for Antony to stay home." *Please, please,* I thought, *let Mrs. Farisee decide we will all stay home.*

I handed the telephone to Aida next, but she didn't say much.

Mrs. Farisee returned with Antony and Preston.

"Oh, wow." Preston stared at my head.

Antony, too, was so struck by my haircut that he kept his eyes on me, while muttering only an occasional "yes" and "no" and "okay" to my father.

"For this, the man made a long distance call?" Mrs. Farisee demanded, when my brother hung up.

His gaze remained fixed on my hair. "Dad wants to know if you're taking us to see the paintings tonight," he told Mrs. Farisee.

She sat down heavily. "I have had glass smashed in my sink, ants loosed in my kitchen, and a morning at the hospital with a frozen parboiled child. As soon as dinner is over, I am going to my room and putting my feet up. I would not leave this house to meet Vincent van Gogh in person."

Though I was preoccupied with my hair, I could see how seriously frazzled Mrs. Farisee was. She had never before given any hint that she was not totally in charge of her world.

"That means you're not taking us?" Antony asked.

My relief was mixed with regret. I'd been looking forward to the van Gogh exhibit. Since its world tour started, magazines and newspapers and radio and television had promoted it. They had convinced me I needed to go; that if I didn't, I would still be regretting the loss at sixty.

The twins had taken no interest in van Gogh until they'd seen a television program which brought up his cutting off his ear. Since then, they'd been fascinated by him.

Reading Mrs. Farisee's narrowed gaze as a confirmed refusal, Antony began negotiating. "How about we go on a bus with Dez? She's almost thirteen."

Mrs. Farisee did not bargain. "Twelve and a half, and she's not taking you twenty miles to a big city and back on a bus at night."

"They could come with us," Preston volunteered.

"My mom's taking my brother and me. She tried to make my father come, but he says he'll be bringing work home from the office. My brother tried to get out of it, too, but my mother won't let him. She told him a chance like this comes once in a lifetime, and when he grows up he'll never forgive her if she lets him pass it by. I'd kind of like to have somebody with us that wants to be there."

"You'll have your mother," Mrs. Farisee reminded him.

"She'll be working in the gift shop. She's a decent."

"You mean a docent," Mrs. Farisee told him.

"Yeah. She said being a museum decent is like being on the symphony guild—it's the way you meet all the people who count. She says that's how you get anywhere, by knowing the people who count. She didn't know she'd have to put in her volunteer time working in the gift shop before she gets to show visitors through the museum and give lectures and stuff." He turned to Antony. "So you guys want to come with us?"

"Mmm." Mrs. Farisee was noncommittal. "You'd have to keep a close eye on the twins, Desdemona."

"I'd just as soon stay home," I told her.

"Then you're not going," Mrs. Farisee told the twins.

"But Preston's mother will take us!" Antony protested.

Mrs. Farisee was unmoved. "If she wants to let

her sons run around a museum unsupervised, that's her business. You two are not going to wander through any exhibit without somebody tending you."

"There'll be such a crowd they're planning to let people through in batches," I ventured. "That means there'll be dozens of decents . . ."

"Docents. They're not going to let volunteer docents handle crowds at an exhibition like this. There'll also be guards. Docents and guards are not there to baby-sit and the subject is closed."

Antony and Aida and Preston looked at me as if I'd banned Christmas. Nobody can gaze at you as bleakly as a five-year-old who feels betrayed.

A horn sounded outside.

"Excuse me." Preston went to the parlor. He was back in a minute. "It's my mother," he told Antony. "I'll ask her, and you get your sister to change her mind."

As Antony took him to get his coat, I heard Preston ask, "Didn't your parents *murder* her for getting her hair all cut off?"

My brother came straight back to the kitchen after he walked Preston to the door. He had to hang around to be sure I knew that he was ignoring me.

Aida sat in the kitchen chair, ignoring all of us.

"Hey, wait a minute." I was indignant. "You guys pour Varathane in the shampoo bottle and make me lose my hair. You scald and freeze your stupid hand and break your ant farm and I'm the one who has to be seen nearly bald with a dumb kid and a wagon full of ants. Now you're mad because I won't take you to a museum?"

Wordlessly, Antony trudged toward our bedroom. Aida headed for the parlor.

"If you charge after them," Mrs. Farisee warned me, "a boot-camp haircut will be the least of your troubles."

I sat down, seething. "They're a whole different generation, do you know that?"

"Every five years is a new generation lately," she observed.

"When I was their age, the Three Stooges gave me nightmares. These kids grow up with preview clips from slasher films flashed at them in the middle of almost every television program. Their idea of a film classic is the original *Night of the Living Dead.* They don't care about van Gogh's art. They care about his ear."

"Put the telephone back and stay away from the twins."

Looping the cord as I walked, I carried the telephone to the rickety hall table, then came back to watch Mrs. Farisee.

With Aida in the parlor and Antony in our room, the only place in the house to avoid them was in the kitchen. If I tried to take refuge in the bathroom, somebody was sure to have to use it.

Mrs. Farisee carried the colander to the kitchen table, put it on a dish towel, and began cracking the string beans. Anybody seeing the cool, decisive precision with which she snapped them would know that she should have been running an army, or at least a corporation. As I sat down across from her, she moved the colander closer to me. "Make yourself useful."

We had cracked most of the beans when Aida wandered into the kitchen. Edging closer to me, she slipped her hand in mine for a second. Then she headed for our bedroom.

"Don't try to forgive me," I yelled after her.

She and my brother came to dinner clean, without even being reminded.

The day had taken a lot out of us all. We ate quietly. Mrs. Farisee was past middle age, and she'd have us on her hands for a weekend that had begun in turmoil and wasn't over yet.

I was thinking about what I would do when Monday morning came.

Antony concentrated on eating, trying to manage with his left hand, using his fork very carefully and having a lot of trouble. His right hand, in a nest of bandages, rested on his lap.

Aida was quiet, too.

You know how a realization opens up for you with no warning. It's not out of the blue, it *is* the blue—a light bright blue that appears, expanding, expanding.

It hit me like that. Suddenly I knew how Aida was feeling. When she was separated from Antony at school, it must have seemed to her that she was losing part of her world. This day, she'd lost him while he was at home with her.

I put down my fork. "Okay. I suppose nobody my age is going to be allowed to go to the city alone at night. Nobody my age is going to risk being seen in public after sundown with a parent, for sure. And nobody, *nobody* from the high school is going to a museum on a Saturday night. How often do I get a chance to herd four little kids through an art exhibit all by myself? I mean, how lucky can I get?"

Five-year-olds do not understand sarcasm or sacrifice, but they were thrilled. The minute we finished dinner, Antony managed to dial Preston's number with his left hand. Having a friend meant even more to my brother than I'd realized. He had the number memorized.

Mrs. Farisee went into the hall to verify with Preston's mother that we were welcome. Then she sent the twins to change clothes while she and I did the dishes.

When we finished, I went to get ready for the museum. The twins were already dressed to go and in the parlor waiting.

Mrs. Farisee's laws were clear and firm. I knew she'd never let me wear slacks to a museum. Even if I wore boots, I'd have to wear knee socks or heavy tights.

I settled for a plaid skirt and pullover sweater with a pair of tan knee socks. I knew that, even if I could bring myself to wear her green-and-orange paisley kerchief, Mrs. Farisee would say it was not warm enough for evening. I tried tying my knit muffler around my skull, but no matter how I arranged it, it left the back of my head bare. Even if I'd had a hooded coat, I would look strange and sinister walking through the exhibit with the hood up. I would certainly be inviting more comments from Preston.

I told myself to think of the evening as a test, to harden me for the ordeal of school.

I went into the parlor. My brother was sitting near the front door. My sister sat on the other side of the room.

"Hey, Antony," I said. "You know your navy blue watch cap?"

"Watch cap?"

"You know. The dark blue knit hat Dad bought you at the surplus store. Do you mind if I wear it?"

He gazed at my hair. "You'd better wear it."

I found the cap where I'd tossed it when I was ransacking the toy box. I pulled the cap down over my ears and looked in the mirror, and was ready to back out of the trip. Then I told myself again sternly that escorting four little kids in a crowd of adults was only a way of working up to the time when I'd have to face my peers. I put on my coat and my rain boots and returned to the parlor just as the front bell rang.

I opened the door myself.

Preston stood on the porch.

Preston was not alone.

"This is my brother Mike," he said.

Mike Harbinger nodded, barely glancing at me.

I started to step back, but Mrs. Farisee and the twins were behind me.

"Don't you let them out of your sight," she cautioned as they squeezed past me, "and keep your hat pulled down over your ears so you don't catch your death. Even a sled dog clipped as close as you are would get chilled."

And I had thought the most harrowing test I had to face was school.

five

Seeing Mike Harbinger on my doorstep was so shattering, it paralyzed any instinct to flee. Silently, I followed the twins and the Harbinger brothers.

There I was, living the fantasy of every girl in my school, walking to a car with Mike Harbinger on a Saturday night.

No one in my class could be warped enough to imagine the fiendish twists given this reality—a Navy surplus watchcap over my stubbled head, three moppets scrambling into the back with me, and a woman in the front seat with an overweight basset hound beside her.

"This must be Anthony and his sisters," she greeted us. "I hope you don't mind if I let Michael drive. He just got his learner's permit, and his father and I want him to have as much practice as possible under our supervision before he's old enough to think about getting his license."

Mrs. Harbinger had the voice of one who has always been sure of her place in life, sure that place is near the top. Her tones were musical, her consonants were crisp, and she didn't bother to wait for answers.

"Check all the mirrors before you pull out," she instructed Mike, then turned her conversation back to the twins and me. "Even though the weather's cleared, I thought it was a good idea to leave early, since, of course, we don't allow Michael to drive on the highways. Actually, I wouldn't let him drive at all after daylight, but we'll take the back roads, and there won't be much traffic. Our town is fair-sized, but I'm afraid it's hardly a cultural mecca. I would imagine most of the crowds at the exhibit will be from the city itself."

Mike drove very slowly, very carefully, under a steady stream of warnings, exhortations, and advice from his mother.

"I hope you don't mind our bringing Wendell," Mrs. Harbinger said, turning her head slightly toward us again.

I wondered if we had yet to pick up Mr. Harbinger.

"If we leave him outside at night," she went on, "he howls so the neighbors complain, and if we keep him shut up inside, he has problems."

"He pees all over the house," Preston confided.

I decided Wendell had to be the dog.

"Preston," Mrs. Harbinger warned. "Wendell's

73

an old dog," she explained, "and he has a little difficulty with his bladder control."

"He can't hold it for more than—"

"Preston." Under those modulated tones lurked the steel of a Mrs. Farisee.

I felt an obligation to say something, since neither the twins nor I had uttered a sound since we got in the car. I might look like a waterfront derelict, I might be out on a Saturday night with my brother and sister, but I didn't want Mike Harbinger thinking I was surly to boot. "Uh ... have you thought of a dog door?" It seemed like a courteous and sensible suggestion.

"We have one, but we keep it locked when we're not home," Mrs. Harbinger said.

"Or else the neighbor's cat gets in and beats up Wendell," Preston added.

Mike Harbinger drove on, silent.

I suppose it takes a long time to recognize something that goes counter to all you expect. It takes even longer when you're preoccupied by your own problems. Very gradually, it occurred to me that Mike Harbinger, who seemed to have had every gift, every advantage, lavished on him, was, right now, a miserably embarrassed fifteen-year-old boy. He was probably feeling so wretched he didn't even suspect how I was suffering.

He probably didn't even notice that I was a girl.

His mother supervised his driving meticulously and unrelentingly. She made him drive through the back streets of the city, and finally she said, "We'll park in that lot up ahead, Michael."

"It's another dozen blocks to the museum, Mom." That was not the voice of a star. This was the voice of everybody who has ever tried to reason with an implacable parent.

"I know what I'm doing, Michael. The lot is supervised, it is well lighted, and I am not going to park with you children on a city street at night. Besides, we'll never find a space any closer."

As the woman at the entrance booth gave Mike a ticket, Mrs. Harbinger leaned toward her. "Will you be good enough to keep an eye on our car? We'll have our basset locked in it."

"Basket?"

"Basset. Basset hound."

"I'm sorry. We can't be responsible for personal property."

Mrs. Harbinger was not ruffled. "He is not property. He is a purebred, registered basset hound." She fished in her purse, and handed Mike a bill. "Give her this, Michael."

I think the parking attendant was overwhelmed, realizing, as I did, that arguing with Mrs. Harbinger was like fighting marshmallow cream. Mike's mother would simply engulf any disagreement in a soft, relentless flow of words.

The attendant took the bill.

"Thank you so much. Go ahead, Michael," Mrs. Harbinger directed.

She told him which space to take, and had him back up twice to ease the car in at the angle she preferred. As she lifted Wendell out, she said, "Be sure you lock all the doors, Michael. And for goodness' sake, don't forget to take the keys. You remember how upset your father was when you locked us all out of the car."

She led Wendell and the rest of us from the parking lot, then handed the end of the leash to Mike. "Take him out to the curb, dear, and be sure he relieves himself."

Wendell plodded after Mike to the curb. The dog's attitude was much like Mike's, weary and resigned. As Wendell lifted his leg, Mike looked off down the street and I gazed the other way.

"There. Put him back in the car, Michael. Don't forget to lock it and leave the window down an inch or two for ventilation."

"I don't think we should leave him," Mike said.

"He'll be perfectly all right for a couple of hours," Mrs. Harbinger replied.

Mike was plainly uncomfortable arguing with her, but he didn't move. "He's old, and it's a cold night."

Preston took up the cause. "Somebody might steal him. The woman can't see him from where she is."

Mrs. Harbinger looked down at her younger son with barely perceptible impatience. "Who is going to steal an ancient basset hound with a bladder condition?"

"You just said he was a purebred registered." While Preston was clearly not happy disagreeing with his mother, neither was he daunted.

"And there are all the fumes from other cars," Mike added. "He already wheezes in his sleep."

"Oh, for heaven's sake!" Mrs. Harbinger snapped. "Bring him, then. I'll just have to keep him in the back of the gift shop and hope nobody makes a fuss." Taking Preston's hand, she strode toward the corner so fast he had to run.

We made an interesting group. Antony trotted beside Preston, pretending, out of natural courtesy, not to notice that Mrs. Harbinger was holding on to her son's hand in public.

Aida walked next to me. I'd never before known her to lag behind her brother.

To my astonishment, Mike fell into step beside us, the dog pottering along behind him. Who would have suspected that this teenage stunner not only stood up for dogs, but didn't scorn strangely dressed twelve-year-old humans? However this night might scar me, I would always remember that Mike Harbinger walked beside me of his own free will.

He didn't speak, of course. He was being dragged to a museum on a Saturday night with his mother, his little brother, a preteener in rain boots and a watch cap, and five-year-old twins, one heavily bandaged and the other heavily depressed.

I suppose, when you're miserable, you're better off not having to endure the company of a jolly, carefree group.

Mrs. Harbinger, however, was not one to let people suffer in peace. She glanced back at Mike. "You see? I was right about the parking. It's barely seven-twenty, and we haven't spotted a single empty space, and all the lots are filled. So," she addressed us all, "how much do we know about Vincent van Gogh?"

Aida looked up at me. Preston looked at the sidewalk. Only a wimp, I knew, would let herself be bullied into reciting everything she knew about van Gogh just to please Mrs. Harbinger. On the other hand, I didn't want to be rude, so I tried to look sincerely interested.

Keeping her grip on Preston, relying upon him not to guide her into the gutter, she looked at Mike and me. "Vincent was born where?"

Never underestimate the power of marshmallow cream. I could not walk on silently when she asked a direct question. "The Netherlands."

"Yes!" In the next few blocks she filled us in on van Gogh's life and a brief history of Postimpressionist painting, without mentioning the severed ear. Nor did she bring up Vincent's onetime friend, Gauguin, who left wife and children and ran off to Tahiti to find himself.

There were hundreds of people in queue for the museum.

"Come along," Mrs. Harbinger told us. "Docents don't wait in line."

The people ahead of us turned to regard her with long, flinty stares.

"Mom, we're not docents." Mike's voice was low. "Everybody else has been standing here...."

"There's no point waiting out here in the cold," Mrs. Harbinger told him.

"I'd rather," he said.

She turned to me.

"I don't mind waiting." While the idea of remaining on display was disheartening, the worst had already happened. Mike had seen me. I didn't have the nerve to sweep past all the people in line. Also, I wasn't convinced that even a docent could whisk us in ahead of them without causing, at the very least, a barrage of hostile comments.

"All right. All right. Then I will just have to freeze out here with you."

"Mom, you don't have to," Mike told her, almost pleading.

"Dear," she said gently, "I am responsible for you all. How would I feel if the twins' mother just turned Preston over to Dorothea at night in the city?"

No self-respecting person can consent to be drowned in marshmallow. "I think the two of us can look after the three of them," I said. "We'll be very careful."

Mike Harbinger might have to endure being seen with a twelve-year-old in a stocking cap. Once he got home, he would probably forget I existed. But at least I was not going to earn his disrespect.

His mother hesitated a moment. "Very well. I will leave you here, then. I'll ask the guards to keep an eye on you, and I want you all to behave. Michael, you and Dorothea must stay right together and hold the little ones by the hand at all times. If anybody has to go to the bathroom, be sure you all go together so you don't get separated."

"Ma!" Preston looked scandalized.

"No, no, no, dear," his mother assured him. "If you or Anthony have to go, Michael will take you both in and Dorothea will wait outside with her sister. And if her sister has to go . . ."

"I know," Aida said politely.

"As soon as the tour is over, you all come directly to the museum gift shop. You may look at things, but you're to handle them carefully and behave like ladies and gentlemen until my shift there ends. Do you understand?"

Preston and Mike nodded.

"Dorothea?"

"Desdemona," I said. "I understand."

After Antony and Aida promised her that they, too, understood, she left us.

Immediately, Preston began talking, as if he had to release all the conversation he'd held in for an hour. Since he talked only to Antony, Aida and Mike and I were left to shuffle in silence toward the head of the line.

Regardless of my father's theories, I could imagine Mike Harbinger being interviewed in fifteen or twenty years. The reporter would ask him about the worst time in his life, and Mike would say, "One Saturday night when I was fifteen, my mother made me take a bunch of kids to a museum." I glanced at him quickly. He was looking straight ahead, stoic. Besides everything else, he had a great profile. *No,* I decided. *No. Dreadful as this evening is, Mike Harbinger has so much going on in his life that, in a year, he'll barely remember it.*

So we edged ahead, Mike herding Preston, Preston talking steadily to Antony, Aida holding my hand. There we were, Mike and Aida and I, with hundreds of people packed around us, each of us totally alone.

It took half an hour of alternately standing still and shuffling forward before we got to the head of the line. Then, for another half hour, we were processed through a maze of red velvet ropes, as if we'd come to the post office during the holiday mailing rush. Once we got into the first room of the van Gogh exhibit, we were left to move on at our own speed.

Mike kept a hand on his brother's shoulder, and Antony stuck close to Preston, so I followed right behind them with Aida.

One Christmas when we lived in California and the twins were just babies, my mother took me to see *The Nutcracker* at the San Francisco Opera House. There were just the two of us, my mother driving, both of us all dressed up, just the two of us together.

I remember looking out the car windows at the traffic in the other lanes, feeling proud that my mother was such a good driver. She wore her good black coat. Her hair was soft and blonde, and in profile she looked like a cameo. I had a red coat with a velveteen collar and new black patent leather shoes. The most important thing was that there were just the two of us.

The Opera House was full, mostly women and the kids they'd brought, all dressed up, to see *The Nutcracker*.

I can even remember how the audience smelled—a blending of bath powder and faint perfumes. At zoos and amusement parks the smell is a hodgepodge of sweat and caramel corn and stale wet diapers. At the Opera House the scents, like the voices, the lights, the colors, the textures of the clothes, were rich and formal, and so exciting it made me dizzy.

We sat in the first balcony, while people found their seats and looked through their programs. It was one of those times that is set so perfectly in your memory that you can bring it all back, the colors, sounds, smells, as if it were still happening.

It was the first ballet I'd ever been to, and with all that *setting,* I knew it was going to be wonderful. In the first minutes, when everything on the stage was a surprise, it was. Then I tried too hard to concentrate on the ballet, so I wouldn't miss anything, so I'd have it all to take home, and probably because I knew I was supposed to appreciate it. I tried so hard my attention cracked, and then wandered, and then I felt guilty.

It was different now, at the van Gogh exhibit. I

was not with my mother. I did not have the certainty that I looked right, and therefore belonged. I was mortified by how wrong I looked. I had layer upon layer of worries.

With so much on my mind, I couldn't concentrate, so I just looked at the paintings. After a while I forgot about the crowd, and how I looked, and how Mike was feeling. There were only the paintings, and the stillness inside when you confront something that's so good it astonishes you.

I started to lift Aida so she could see better, but she twitched away like a cat that doesn't want to be carried. We moved on in a crush of people.

"Hey, wow!" Preston said to Antony. "Look at those stars! I bet that's just how stars look if you're nearsighted."

And Aida made her move.

From her pocket, she took the bag of carob chips she'd bought that morning, and held them out to Preston. "Want some?"

It was so fine, the kind of gesture that probably helped lift our whole species from savagery. Instead of cherishing her hurt, or being rotten, she held out that bag to the enemy.

And I had to slap down her great gesture. There were signs all over forbidding food and drink. "Aida, you're not allowed . . ."

"Eeeyeww!" Preston drew back. *"Ants!"*

Besides its phenomenal staying power, Preston's voice carried.

As people followed his gaze, the polite murmuring that had surrounded us was rippled by muted exclamations of dismay. All we needed was Bramwell Grove to stir up the crowd with reminders of Charlton Heston and the army ants.

I couldn't hustle Aida to a bathroom. There was no hurrying through a crush like this, and I certainly didn't want to shove my sister and her bag of ant-covered carob chips at people who were already edgy. Besides, tossing ants in the bathroom's trash container would certainly get them killed.

I took the knit glove off my left hand, snatched the bag from Aida, and stuffed it into the glove.

The people who had been nearest us moved ahead as quickly as they could.

Though I was tempted to shake off the ants crawling up my fingers, I picked them off carefully, flicked them gently into the glove, and held the wrist closed, knowing the occupants would be finding their way out before long.

Mike Harbinger watched me as if he were witnessing a bizarre but fascinating ritual.

I forced myself to speak directly to him. "You wouldn't have a rubber band or anything?"

He shook his head. "Maybe we'd better go."

People who had been behind us were edging around us, cautiously.

"Not before we see the picture where his ear's cut off," Antony protested.

"*Ear's cut off?*" Preston's voice again drew the attention of everyone around us.

Being far below adult eye level, and concerned with something irresistibly gruesome, Preston had no idea of the effect he was creating. *"Ear's cut off? Whose?"*

"Van Gogh's, and shut up," Mike told him.

Preston was too shocked and excited to worry about keeping his voice down. "Somebody cut off *van Gogh's* ear? Who?"

"Van Gogh," Mike said, trying to move him through the crowd.

There is no way to budge a kid who is consumed by an urgent need to know something. *"I mean, who cut off his ear?"*

"Van Gogh cut off van Gogh's ear." Mike got a firmer grip on his brother.

"HE CUT OFF HIS OWN EAR? THAT'S WORSE THAN FREEZING OFF YOUR HAND!" Preston cried.

Antony gazed at his bandaged arm. *"Freeze it off?"*

"That's enough!" As I reached for my brother, I dropped the ant-filled glove.

"My ants!"

Aida dived for the glove.

Hauling her up, I grabbed Antony and dragged them past years of van Gogh's work.

Luckily, this was a museum crowd, made up, except for us, of people with respect for culture and civilization. Even their annoyance was restrained as we squirmed and struggled toward the green EXIT sign.

85

As I reached it, two guards flanking the door stepped forward. "I'm sorry," one told me. "Would you mind going . . ."

"We've got a glove full of ants here." Mike Harbinger, behind me, put his hand on my shoulder.

He actually put his hand on my shoulder. Mike Harbinger did.

". . . Ants?"

"A swarm," Mike assured the guard.

The second guard opened the door. "Don't try coming back," he said as I ushered the twins through.

I strode across the pavement, so paranoid I didn't dare run for fear it might look as if I'd used the ants to cover our theft of a van Gogh.

The minute I reached the bushes, I grabbed the glove from my sister.

Holding it by one finger, I shook out the bag so the ants wouldn't be trapped. I tucked glove and bag under a cotoneaster, then blew a few ants off my fingers.

Preston, with Mike and the twins, stood watching.

"You're littering," he said.

I reminded myself that, however he resembled his mother, he was only five years old, and short at that. "Preston—Preston, there is nothing else to do with a glove full of ants and candy. Have you ever tried to get ants out of a knit glove, Preston? You want me to carry that glove around the streets *all night* looking for a trash can? You want those ants,

86

who have lived up to now in an ant farm, to be dumped in a trash can and picked up and *crushed* in a trash masher? You want me to bring them in your mother's car?"

Preston did not abash easily. "If my mother finds out we're wandering around here at night, she'll have a cow. And, boy, when she finds out you just about started a riot in there...."

"*I* started a riot? If you hadn't started yelling about cut-off ears and hands, Preston—"

Mike drew his brother back from my wrath. "We'd better go around front and wait for my mom."

"Yeah," Preston told me. "Before you're picked up for disturbing the peace."

While standing by the side exit of a museum at night yelling at a five-year-old was no crime, I couldn't be sure that somebody we'd offended inside hadn't complained.

We walked around to the front of the building.

"I don't think we'd better try to go in again," I told Mike.

"I would not take any of these three in there again for anything," he said flatly.

I was still apprehensive. "Do you think we look suspicious hanging around outside here?"

"Act casual," Preston advised.

"I'd better go in and tell my mother where we are," Mike decided.

"She said we were absolutely to stick together," Preston reminded him.

I had to agree with this kid who could have turned Mother Teresa against the human race. "She did. And she was . . . very firm."

"I guess she'll know we're out here." Mike stood with one foot on the sidewalk, one on the lowest step, his back against a pedestal with a copy of Rodin's *The Thinker* on it. Just *standing,* Mike Harbinger was a study in how to look terrific.

And I realized that I hadn't thought about how he looked or who he was for . . . well, close to half an hour. What he had been, all along, was a person you'd want around in an emergency.

He cleared his throat. "So . . . how did the ants get from the farm into your sister's coat pocket?"

I told him about that morning, about the ant farm and Antony's burned hand and relocating the ants. The story was harrowing, even now. Still, I did not mention my hair. Even when your audience is enthralled, you do not call attention to the fact that you are almost bald.

"What are you doing out here?" Mrs. Harbinger came hurrying down the museum steps. Her voice could have shattered a museum chandelier. "I told you you were to come directly to the gift shop!"

"We . . . had to leave," Mike said.

"That's no excuse! You deliberately disobeyed me, every one of you, and I could have been worried *sick!*"

"I'm sorry." Mike sounded sincere, but not intimidated. "I didn't think you'd want us all hanging around in there too long."

88

"You didn't think! You didn't think at all. I am furious, Michael!"

I could hardly stand by and let him take the blame. "Actually, it was my—"

"I don't want to hear another word about it! I even had to leave the dog back in there."

"Do you want me to go get him?" Mike asked.

"I do not want any one of you moving one inch from this spot until I come back. Not an inch!" Mrs. Harbinger walked around to the side of the museum, her high heels punishing the pavement.

None of us spoke.

There are few things more embarrassing than being with somebody whose mother has just jumped all over him. You're too ashamed to say anything until enough time has passed that you can act as if it never happened and change the subject. Despite my discomfort, I was aware that Mike Harbinger, besides being gorgeous, athletic, smart, and nice, had more class than anybody I knew, except my father. I didn't deepen his humiliation, of course, by saying anything about his taking the blame for us all.

Even Preston showed some sense by keeping quiet.

Of course, Mrs. Harbinger hadn't berated him.

We didn't know one another well enough, or have the presence of mind, to dredge up a change of subject. The longer the silence went on, the more strained it would have seemed to say anything to break it. Instead, we stood around, trying to look interested in the museum architecture, or absorbed in private thoughts.

Mrs. Harbinger returned, leading Wendell. By then she'd gone from indignation to silent disapproval. We all walked back to the car without talking, standing mute each time Wendell stopped to wet a bush or a street sign.

At the car, Mike unlocked the door on his mother's side first and lifted Wendell in.

On the way home, Mrs. Harbinger broke the silence. As before, she coached Mike's driving: warning, advising, correcting, but in a low, flat, cold voice. She didn't ask how we liked the exhibit, or try to tell us more about van Gogh.

Aida fell asleep, leaning against me. When she started to snore, I let her. Mike and his mother couldn't think any worse of us.

When we stopped at our house, I nudged my sister awake and said "Thank you" to Mrs. Harbinger. Prompted by her, Mike got out and opened the car door and walked the twins and me to the porch.

"Thanks," I said.

He nodded. " 'Night."

Mrs. Farisee was in the parlor reading a paperback, which she tucked into the pocket of her robe as we entered. "Did you have a nice time?"

"If I had a diary," I told her, "I'd burn it."

six

Sherman didn't come over until long after church on Sunday. He came to the back door, as usual.

"I was beginning to think you'd decided to stick around your own home long enough to get acquainted with it," Mrs. Farisee greeted him, then took the newspaper back to her room.

"I had to get out of there," he told me. "They made me straighten my whole room and wash Jake, and they're still in a cleaning frenzy."

"On a Sunday?" I wondered whether Mrs. Farisee had taken the television section with her.

"It's the party."

"What party?" I was glad to see she'd left the comics section on the kitchen table.

"My parents' big party to announce my dad's running for mayor. I told you." He didn't seem aggrieved that I'd forgotten. I suppose it happened to him often. "They had to invite all the important

91

people who'd be insulted if he didn't tell them he was running for mayor before he announces that he is."

"You mean they don't know it? Everybody says your father is going to run for mayor. It's in the paper all the time."

"Sure, everybody knows, but he hasn't *announced* it. He has to tell all the important people at one time so they won't get mad because he told somebody else first. He has to tell them, and then Monday he's holding a press conference to announce it. And, boy—are my parents tense! Our maid quit yesterday because my mother was driving her crazy, and then we couldn't find a cleaning service to come in at the last minute."

"Your house is always clean. Your house is immaculate."

"Listen, before a party they even have the windowsills waxed. I think they're afraid somebody will sneak a look into my room or get a whiff of the dog bed and decide we're not perfect. Of course, they're extra stressed because they have to invite my uncle Bramwell. He kind of undermines the way they want people to see us. He's like unwaxed sills or clutter under the bed."

"Why don't they present him like a diamond in the rough?"

"My uncle," Sherman said flatly, "is a mine field in the rough. They don't dare not invite him—he's got more money than they'll ever have. Besides, if he didn't come, everybody would be wondering why."

"Doesn't anybody like him?"

Sherman was thoughtful. "You know, in a way I almost do. He drives my parents crazy."

Mrs. Farisee refused to let Sherman come with us to pick up my father. "I am paid to look after three children, not to cart their friends everywhere I go."

I dreaded taking my head out in public again, but she wouldn't let me stay home. "I do not plan to return and find that somebody has put motor oil in the mayonnaise jar, and I am not taking two five-year-olds without you to help keep them quiet."

At the airport, Mrs. Farisee told me I could not wait in the car.

"I'll keep the windows up and the doors locked," I promised.

"Come."

Walking through the airport, I kept the watch cap pulled way over my ears.

The minute Antony and Aida spotted our father, they were all over him. Immediately, Aida started telling him about Antony's hand, and the ants. She did not mention my hair or my haircut, the ride with Bramwell, or the trip to the museum.

With all Aida's breathless talking, my father didn't have a chance to ask me why I was looking like a merchant seaman braving a sou'wester.

There must be an amnesia that affects us sometime in our teens. Little kids are a hundred times more observant, and more sensitive, than adults choose to recall. My sister was spilling over, recounting Antony's accident and the ant farm adventure in riveting detail. Probably without even trying, she edited out all the parts she and Antony and I wouldn't want our father to know.

When we got home, I kept the cap on, but nobody noticed.

My father had brought us all presents, even a clock radio for Mrs. Farisee. I could see she was pleased. She had an alarm clock and her own radio and television set, but it was nice that he thought of her as someone who might like waking to music.

The minute we'd unwrapped our gifts, Antony asked, "Can Preston come over?"

"*May* Preston come over," my father said automatically. There's a certain security in little things like that. A parent who has never yet gotten his kid to say *may* instead of *can* never stops trying. "Who's Preston?"

"My friend."

"Oh! Sure. So long as I don't have to pick him up." As soon as Antony went to telephone Preston, my father asked me, "What's this friend like?"

"I am not in a position to give an unbiased opinion."

"He is a perfect little gentleman," Mrs. Farisee said, "and you may not wear that stocking cap all day and all night in the house, Desdemona." She left the room.

I didn't wait for my father to ask questions. "Let me tell you about my hair before you see it, and please don't say anything when you do see it, because if you do I know I'll cry."

Being a psychologist, of course, he was good at listening. He sat quietly, giving me all his attention, while I explained about the varnish and the Mona Lisa. Before I knew it, I was telling about Mike Harbinger and everything that happened at the museum, and finally about Bramwell and Shirley and the dog.

When I finished, he shook his head and muttered "Oh, boy," as if he understood just how it had been and just how I felt. I was sure that if I asked him in a week, he could repeat everything I'd told him without missing anything important.

Finally, I took off the cap. My father looked at my hair solemnly. I was glad he didn't try to tell me it looked okay, or remind me that it would grow out.

The telephone rang, which was just as well. I'd been telling him my problems without even giving him a chance to call Shirley.

Mrs. Farisee opened the door from the hall. "Sherman's on the line, Desdemona."

Sherman sounded ill at ease. "My mother made me call," he told me. "She wants to borrow you."

"*Borrow* me?"

"That's how she put it. She leaned so hard on the caterer's crew that they all walked out. The caterer is hanging in there by a thread. There's nobody to help him and to take coats and empty ashtrays, except me."

"Sherman, does she know how my hair looks?"

"Right now my parents would accept you if you'd tattooed your skull. They'll just keep you in the kitchen."

When I hesitated, he went on. "Look, I don't want to tell you what to do. But if I were renting a house from them and had three dogs and no lease and no place else to go, I think I'd..."

"I know."

"On the one hand, it's blackmail. On the other hand, I'm thinking of you and the dogs out in the cold even before the condo deal."

"Tell her yes."

"Good. I didn't want to push you, Dez, but I need a friend here, too."

"What do I wear?"

"A dress, but nothing so fancy you look like company."

"When?"

"Soon as you can. The party starts at four."

Though I dreaded taking my head out, even to the Groves' kitchen, I knew Sherman was right.

I went back to my father. "Sherman's parents are stuck. They're having a big party, and everybody but the caterer has walked out on them. They asked if I could come help."

"You want to?"

"Sure." I couldn't let him know I was doing it because I didn't dare risk the Groves' ill will. Should he have to face the knowledge that his daughter was going to work in the landlord's kitchen to delay her family's being thrown out on the streets?

Mrs. Farisee made me eat before I left. She knew what she was doing. Sherman's parents would never have invited me or anybody in my family as a guest. At least I wouldn't get hungry while I was there. If they offered me food, I could honestly say, "No, thanks. I've eaten."

I owned three winter dresses. Since the Groves would keep me in the kitchen, I chose the coolest one.

Mrs. Farisee came into the bedroom with the scarf she'd worn to church. It was either silk or a good imitation. "This is a little more respectable," she said. "Try tying it with the knot behind your head. It might look more dressy."

My father drove me to the Groves'.

"I hope they won't want me to take the scarf off in the house," I said.

"Did I ever tell you about my stepfather's aunt?"

"I don't know." I could not have been less interested in stories about his relatives. In my mind, I was rehearsing what I would say if Mrs. Grove told me to take the scarf off my head. I could say I was coming down with something, which might very well be true, but then she might be annoyed with me for bringing germs into the house. I could say I thought it would be more sanitary if I'd be handling food. Then she might be offended that I took it upon myself to tell her what was sanitary.

My father talked on, ignoring my lack of attention. "I was eight or ten when I first met her. She must have been over sixty. Even at my age, I could tell she wore a wig. Either it wasn't a very good wig, or the fact that she had no eyebrows or eyelashes was the tip-off. She'd lost every hair, even on her arms and legs, when she was in her teens."

"How?" I was so startled I forgot my own train of thought.

"Scarlet fever, diphtheria—I'm not sure. Something kids don't get anymore. But her hair never grew back."

"This is supposed to cheer me up?"

He didn't smile, but he wasn't ruffled. "Do you want to strike a pose or admit that you'll have a decent head of hair in a few months?"

"This is supposed to make me feel shallow for taking a mere scalping so hard." I was not going to admit that I wanted to hear more about his stepfather's aunt.

He went on as if I hadn't interrupted. "She never married. Besides being bald, she was nearly six feet tall, and this was generations ago, remember. She had a long face and great wonderful sad eyes like Virginia Woolf's, but unfortunately she did not have Virginia Woolf's elegant nose."

By this time, I was thoroughly engrossed. "Who's Virginia Woolf?"

"A writer. As a matter of fact, in the twenties and thirties she wrote about the need of women for independence and the freedom to be creative. Anyway, Serena, my stepfather's aunt, had a magnificent nose. It would have looked splendid on an aging Roman emperor. In profile, she resembled an eagle, and if you say bald eagle, you may walk the rest of the way to the Groves'."

"Go on." I was so wrapped up in Serena's story, I wasn't even indignant at the suggestion that I might joke about her.

"She was a recluse. I would guess that when she was young, her parents kept her tucked away to protect her, since she looked so dramatically different from what was considered to be acceptable for a woman." He stopped at an intersection, and, while his eyes were on the road, I realized he was seeing her somewhere in his mind.

Gazing at his profile, I noticed that his own hair was already thinning at the temples. He wasn't handsome like Harley or Bramwell Grove, but he was a very presentable man. He looked like a person who thought a lot, and worried, and was kind and decent, and I was glad he was my father. I was even glad he'd gone back to wearing his glasses; contact lenses reminded me of the phase after my mother left when he was dating women who looked like the extras in MTV videos.

"But you didn't meet this aunt until she was over sixty?" I asked, to remind him he was talking to me.

He nodded, and drove on. "I used to love visiting her. She was a cultured woman: brilliant, gentle, well read. Most of all, she had a generous heart, a generous spirit. Her instincts must have been fine to begin with, so her judgment was humane and original. When I was thirty, and she couldn't get around without a walker, I realized I'd been in love with her for years."

"In love?"

He nodded. "That, my child, is how our age has cheated you. I'm not talking about the kind of love that sells paperbacks and movie tickets. You can be in love without any kind of physical desire."

I could understand what he meant. On the other hand, I could see that writers or filmmakers who dealt with that kind of love were not likely to have enormous audiences. I wondered if any of them would ever dare present a heroine like Serena.

"It's a dirty trick," he said, "to convince the young that they're worthless unless they look like models, with bodies perfected by Nautilus machines, makeup hiding every flaw."

"If you meant to make me feel better, did you kind of wander off the subject?" I asked.

"No. I meandered through it."

A wide circular driveway led to the Groves' front door. Along the sides and back of the lot were towering Italian cypresses, almost trunk to trunk.

"Call me when you're ready to leave," my father said. "I'm going to swing by Shirley's. If I'm not home, I'll be there."

"I was wondering when you were going to get around to her."

"I called her while you were dressing, but first her line was busy and then there was no answer. She's probably back home by now."

He let me out and drove on.

As I walked up the driveway to the front entrance, I heard a car pull in and stop.

Mrs. Grove must have been waiting for any sign of help, because she answered the door herself. "Desdemona, thank heavens!" She was still in her robe. Sherman, beside her, wore a white shirt, dark trousers, and a necktie.

"Let me collect my thoughts, Desdemona." Mrs. Grove pressed delicate fingers to her temples. "It's going to be a matter of where we need you most." While she looked distraught, she was not disheveled. Her robe was a dark wine-colored velvet, and her high-heeled slippers were purple satin.

As the people from the car came up the steps, she stopped talking. Sherman stared past me in astonishment.

"Hey, Sherman. Dez." It was Shirley Miller's voice.

I turned.

Shirley Miller stood there with Mona and Lisa—and Bramwell Grove.

I tried to speak, but I could only nod. Sherman's "Oh. Hi," sounded as surprised as I felt.

Mrs. Grove recovered her voice, if not her manners. "It's a nightmare," she greeted Bramwell.

"The fireplace is belching, *belching* smoke and ash, and Harley is in there making it worse. The dog has taken a violent dislike to the caterer. The downstairs bathroom is backed up, which means, of course, that it's going to affect the rest of the house, and we can't get a plumber." Her glance kept straying to Mona and Lisa.

Mona wore a short, imitation leopard Orlon coat over her pink uniform. Lisa's coat was made of white fake fur. She and Mona gazed at Mrs. Grove stoically, like prisoners determined not to crack under interrogation.

"You know Shirley Miller," Bramwell said.

Sherman's mother managed to focus on Shirley and to smile without moving anything but her lips. "Shirley. What a pleasant surprise."

"And Mona and Lisa," Bramwell added.

Mrs. Grove really looked at them then—as if she were certain they'd come to the wrong house.

"They were good enough to come help you out of your mess," Bramwell prompted his sister-in-law.

Her face remained fixed in that smile. "How very kind. Sherman, take the ladies back to the maid's room and show them where to leave their wraps."

I smiled at Shirley, feeling sheepish that I'd even imagined she'd come with Bramwell socially. Nevertheless, I didn't trust the man's intentions. He stood too close to her, for one thing.

Since I wasn't sure whether I was included among the "ladies," I stood waiting for instructions from Mrs. Grove.

Mona and Lisa stepped into the foyer and followed Sherman down the hall. Shirley didn't.

Mrs. Grove kept smiling until Mona and Lisa were out of earshot. Then she asked Bramwell, her voice quiet but intense, "Who are they?"

"Mona and Lisa."

"I mean, who *are* they?"

"The only people I could put the arm on to work at your shindig on an hour's notice. And they have uniforms."

"*Pink nylon?* Pink nylon uniforms with white orthopedic wedgies?"

"They're hairdressers! What do you want? You want me to pop by the mortuary and see if any of their embalmers are free?"

A howl came from Bramwell's car.

"There. Now you've got my dog upset."

"Your dog! What dog?" Mrs. Grove demanded.

"Shirley found him, and now I'm stuck with him," Bramwell said. "He's ... attached to me. I can't go from one room to another without him at my heels. Smartest little guy you'd ever want to meet. Just this morning he—"

"I'd better reassure him." Shirley hurried off to the car.

"I don't appreciate you pulling your snob routine in front of my date," Bramwell told Mrs. Grove in a low voice. "I would like her to think this family has a little more class."

I had to stand there. I could not humiliate my father or myself by letting these people see how I felt.

Only a minute ago I had been ashamed of doubting Shirley!

Mrs. Grove glanced at me. "You go on back to the kitchen, Desdemona. The caterer can tell you what to do." Then she coughed. Behind her the foyer was beginning to look hazy, and I could smell the smoke.

Walking down the hall to the back of the house, I thought of my father, driving over to Shirley's apartment, maybe even waiting around for her.

Sherman was standing outside the maid's room, his back against the wall. "I don't think those women want to be here," he confided.

I knew I'd better not try to speak until I had my feelings under control. I went into the maid's room. Mona was peering in the mirror, wiping something off her tooth with her little finger.

I put my coat on the bed with the leopard Orlon and the white acrylic.

Lisa came out of the bathroom adjusting her bra straps. "Up and at 'em," she said bleakly.

"Hey," Mona reminded me as I started for the hall, "you still have your scarf on your head."

I couldn't tell them I was hiding their work. I took it off.

As I came out of the maid's room with Mona and Lisa, Sherman got his first look at my haircut. His eyes widened and his mouth opened, and then he collected himself. "Well. Um ... Well. I guess we'd better go to the kitchen."

The Groves' kitchen was enormous. Under a window was a long stainless steel sink flanked by yards of tiled counters and wooden cabinets. Beside the six-burner range against a side wall were two ovens plus a microwave suspended under a cabinet. Even the refrigerator was oversized. In the center of the room was a work island, with dozens of fancy bowls and trays and platters on its butcher-block top. A three-tier serving cart stood next to the island.

The kitchen had three doors—the one we came through, a back door to the laundry room, and a swinging door that led into the dining room. A thread of smoke was wisping in around the swinging door.

A tall, heavy man in a dark suit and white apron stood at the sink. Despite the cold, the window in front of him was open.

On the counter at his left were stacks and stacks of tiny bread slices, ranging from pale cream color to dark, dark brown. Behind the bread were more than a dozen boxes of crackers, brands I'd never seen on a supermarket shelf. The counter on his right looked like a display of loot from a gourmet deli robbery—jars, cans, bottles, little crockery tubs, boxes of fancy toothpicks, an array of knives and openers.

"This is our caterer," Sherman told us.

Mona and Lisa looked around the kitchen, wary as zebras picking their way to a crocodile-infested water hole.

Sherman addressed the caterer's back. "These are Miss Mona and Miss Lisa, and Desdemona Blank."

The caterer turned. His gaze swept from Mona's and Lisa's hair over their shiny pink uniforms to their orthopedic shoes, and then from my shoes up to my hair. A muscle under his left eye twitched.

"He's running a few hours behind schedule," Sherman explained.

"What do you want us to do?" Mona asked.

"Peel the shrimp," the caterer said.

"Peel the shrimp," Mona repeated to Lisa, but her tone said, *Didn't I tell you?*

The door from the dining room swung open. Mrs. Grove, in stocking feet, wearing a shimmering blue dress that looked fragile as butterfly wings, swept in, along with a smoky haze. Moving the caterer aside, she bent to open the cupboard doors under the sink and stick her head in. After a moment, she backed out, yelling, "It isn't in there!"

From the parlor came Mr. Grove's strangled shout, "Try the garage!"

Rising, Sherman's mother tiptoed out the back door.

The caterer waved his hands, trying to dispel the smoke. He turned back to the sink and shut the cupboard doors with his knee.

Then he jerked his head toward a colander full of shrimp that stood in the sink. "You clean them and shell them and arrange them appealingly on a platter," he told Mona, as he began opening containers arrayed on the counter.

Mona stepped up to the sink, and I eased over until I was far to the caterer's right, with my back against a counter. It seemed like a good idea to stay out of the traffic lanes.

Mrs. Grove came in from the laundry room. Before she could block him, Jake scurried past her. With a growl like a rat's gargle, he began savaging the caterer's trouser leg. The man did not move. He had probably heard somewhere that you should never run from an attacking animal.

"For heaven's sake, feed the dog!" Mrs. Grove commanded Sherman distractedly. Then she noticed my hair. "Oh, my word!"

"Where is the blessed plunger?" Mr. Grove yelled.

"It has to be in one of the bathrooms!" Mrs. Grove shouted, as she rushed out the door to the maid's room.

Sherman pried Jake from the caterer's trouser leg and handed the writhing, snarling beast to me.

"Excuse me," Sherman said. "I need the dog food." Squeezing past the caterer, he climbed up on the counter. His heel hit a jar, and olives and juice cascaded over the tiles.

"That does it." The caterer tore off his apron, threw it on the floor and strode past me and out the back door.

Mrs. Grove came in the side door, looking harried. "I *know* we have a plunger. There has got to be one in this house." She spied the apron on the floor. "That is absolutely uncalled for. That is totally unsanitary." She snatched it up and tossed it over a food processor. "Tell the caterer he's going to have to get some food out before the guests come," she instructed Sherman.

"I think he . . . left," Sherman said.

"Left? What for? How could a man who calls himself a professional run out of anything at this hour?"

Sherman climbed down off the counter, avoiding jars and juice and olives. "I don't think he's coming back."

Rushing to the back door, Mrs. Grove yanked it open.

She screamed.

"I'm sorry! I didn't mean to scare you." Mike Harbinger stood in the doorway, wearing slacks and jacket.

I should not have been surprised. Why should I have been surprised?

It was not only inevitable, it was necessary. I had shared hours of shame and misery with Mike Harbinger the evening before, but he had not seen my uncovered head. What is fate for, if not to give you one last kick when you think it has tired of abusing you?

Mrs. Grove's scream had roused Jake's feral instincts. As he struggled to get free, Mike looked at him. "Hey, dog."

108

It was too late to run. Mike looked at my hair. He looked me in the eyes, then he looked back at my hair. It took him only an instant to master his astonishment. "Hi," he told me. Then he turned his gaze back to Mrs. Grove. "Nobody answered the front door. I'm Mike Harbinger. My mom sent me over early. She said you needed help."

To slink out of the kitchen, I would have to cross it, or squeeze past Mike, or enter the Groves' dining room where I might see Shirley and Bramwell. There was no point, anyway. Mike had seen my hair. If I tried to slip away, Mrs. Grove would probably send him to fetch me. I could only stand and suffer.

Outside, a car engine started.

"Stop the caterer!" Mrs. Grove ordered Mike.

"Ma'am?"

Shoving him aside, she ran out the back door.

Mike looked at me. "Did I say something?" Then he sniffed. "I think you have a fire."

"We know," Sherman told him. "We're working on it."

Mike hesitated, then said to Sherman, Mona, and Lisa, "I'm Mike Harbinger."

Through the open kitchen window, I heard Sherman's mother discussing things with the caterer. He matched her shriek for shriek, then drove off.

"Was this a bad time to show up?" Mike asked me.

He stepped aside as Mrs. Grove marched in the back door. "A man who has no patience with dogs

109

and children should not be allowed to deal with the public." She looked around the room. "What has he been doing?" Stepping to the counter at the right of the sink, she ripped a few paper towels from a holder. She blotted the olive juice, then used the soaked towels to sweep the olives into the sink.

Mona snatched the colander of shrimp out of her way.

Shirley came through the swinging door. She was wearing a swirling gray dress with a low neckline. "I've got the fireplace under control. Is it safe to wash up in here?" Then she saw my hair. She stood for a second, transfixed.

"The caterer has abandoned us." Mrs. Grove did have a flair for making announcements rather than mere statements. "The guests will be arriving at any moment. The plumbing is still backed up, and I am thinking of leaving myself."

"You'd better put some shoes on and greet people." Shirley stepped over to the sink and turned on the faucets. "I'll help in here."

Mrs. Grove marched to the swinging door like Marie Antoinette to the guillotine, shoved it open, and stepped through.

I stood there, still holding Jake. It was not enough for fate to trap me at this party with a shorn head and Mike Harbinger. Impossible though it seemed, things had taken a turn for the worse. Now, I had to work in the same kitchen with a woman who had dumped my unsuspecting father for a rich slumlord.

Shirley finished rinsing her hands and turned to me. "Why are you holding that dog, Dez?" she asked. She didn't even seem uncomfortable talking to the daughter of the man she had betrayed.

"I forgot," Sherman said. "I'm supposed to feed him."

"Better get it done, then," Shirley advised him.

As Sherman climbed up on the counter again, Mona lifted the colander out of his way and stepped back. Shirley eased over to the right-hand counter and moved containers away from Sherman's feet.

Putting the colander in the sink once more, Mona resumed shrimp peeling.

Shirley surveyed the array of bottles and cans and tubs and jars on the counter. She turned to Mike. "Why don't you start bringing some platters over?"

Lisa stood before the stacks of bread and crackers looking like somebody waiting in line to pay a bill. "I'll start passing stuff over," Shirley told her. "You can start constructing hors d'oeuvres."

Lisa glanced at Mona, who went on peeling shrimp.

At the center island, Mike began stacking platters.

Shirley peered into a few of the tubs. "Dip. Okay. We'll need bowls for those."

Mike stacked bowls on the platters.

"Wowee! Truffles." Shirley picked up a tiny can. "Your dad must have the election in the bag, Sherman."

111

Sherman looked down at the can. "Truffles are a fungus, right?"

"Keep in mind that mushrooms are, too." Shirley stuck the can under the electric opener.

"Truffles grow underground and pigs dig them up," Sherman added.

"And people pay five hundred dollars a pound for them." Shirley opened a can of mushroom pâté and a jar of pimientos. "As a matter of fact, only a caterer can afford a can as big as the one I opened."

Mona looked at the truffles and then at Lisa. Lisa looked at the truffles, then at Mona. I wondered how many days' rent, theirs or ours, were in those few ounces of fungus.

Shirley went on opening cans and jars and bottles.

As Mike carried a stack of platters to Lisa, she cleared a place on the counter for them.

I was still holding Jake.

Sherman surveyed the top shelf. "Let's see. He had that yesterday. He's tired of that. That he won't eat." Finally he handed a can of dog food down to Shirley. "Would you open this for me?"

"Sure."

As she opened the can, Jake began struggling to get at it.

"Hey, come on." Mike sauntered over to me and stroked Jake's head. "You're a nice little guy," Mike told him.

Jake kissed his hand.

It was too much for me. Handing the dog to Mike, I stood back from all the action.

Mona lifted the colander to rinse off the shrimp.

"Snake!" Bramwell Grove shouted, as he came through the side door.

Bags and boxes fell out of the cupboard as Sherman grabbed a shelf. Shirley dropped the can of dog food and held his leg to steady him. Mona threw her hands in the air, along with the colander. Lisa yelled. I looked around for something we could coax a snake into.

"Hey! Hey! Keep it down! You're getting crazy in here," Bramwell admonished. "Sherman, check the garage for a snake."

Bracing her hands on the counter, Shirley closed her eyes for a moment. Then she spoke very carefully. "He means he wants a plumber's snake, Sherman. A plumber's snake is a long piece of metal for cleaning drains. You may find it coiled up, hanging on the wall in your garage. That is where a plumber's snake is kept in your average household."

Bramwell stared at my hair. "Oh." His *oh* was that of a man who has seen a grievous thing. He looked at Mona and Lisa, who were picking shrimp off the counters. "You let a little girl talk you into doing that? Don't you people have any sense of responsibility?"

I was too outraged to speak, even to defend Mona and Lisa. Here was the man basically responsible

113

for my Varathaned hair, accusing the people who had tried to help me deal with it.

Shirley helped Sherman off the counter and fished cans and jars and bags and boxes out of the scatter of shrimp in the sink.

"Listen," Bramwell told Mona and Lisa. "You two run interference out there. One of you take the first floor, the other the upstairs. Head off anybody who tries to use a bathroom."

"Bramwell," Shirley protested.

"You want me to send one of the kids to do it?" With his jacket off and his sleeves up, Bramwell looked especially dashing, like some rich landowner who's been rounding up his horses before the tropical hurricane strikes. "The press will be here any minute. How would it look across the front page: Plumbing Erupts, Disrupts . . ."

"Never mind," Shirley said wearily.

"This has got to be it." Sherman staggered in, dragging a great coil of metal, thicker than my thumb and ten or twelve feet long. He lurched across the kitchen to his uncle, the snake scraping the floor.

Bramwell hoisted the snake to his own shoulder effortlessly. "Okay, ladies. Front and center."

Mona and Lisa followed Bramwell, leaving a floor littered with shrimp.

Recalling that I had actually mentioned the man's name in the beauty shop, I realized I'd been lucky to get off with nothing worse than the haircut I had.

114

"Do you have a laundry tub?" Shirley asked Sherman.

"Sure," he said.

"Why don't you scrub your hands out there, and then feed your dog—out there. I'd better go help with the plumbing."

She left, and Mike tried to calm Jake, who was struggling to get at the shrimp.

"How can she?" I exploded. "How *can* she?"

"Bram's an artist," Sherman said. "I've seen him collect rents. What he does is keep people off balance. One minute he's . . ."

"Unbearable," I said.

"He projects . . ."

"Obnoxiousness."

"Confidence," Sherman went on, "as if there's no question but that he's going to get what he wants, no matter who's in the way. The next minute, he's charming, so that nobody can keep up with his changes."

"Can't she *see*?" I demanded.

"Of course she sees," Sherman told me. "That's what makes him so interesting, if you're not doing business with him. A wolf is more intriguing than a dog."

"Thanks. Thanks a lot," I said.

"Come on, Dez. I didn't mean that."

Mike shifted his grip on Jake. "When are you going to feed this dog?"

"Let him eat shrimp," I snapped.

"That is rotten, really rotten." Sherman began

115

collecting shrimp off the floor. "Just because Shir-ley dumps your father, you take it out on my dog."

"I don't think one or two shrimp would hurt him," Mike ventured.

"He's not used to them." Sherman stood and threw a handful of shrimp into the sink. "They could upset his stomach."

They could, I realized, and I was instantly ashamed. You don't make smart cracks about any-thing that could hurt a dog.

Maneuvering Jake under one arm, Mike stroked him with his free hand. "That was very good, how you figured that character out," he told Sherman.

"Character?" Sherman knelt to pick up a few more shrimp.

"Your uncle. Bramwell. The slumlord," I told Sherman.

What am I saying? I thought. *How can I be so nasty?*

Sherman stood and dropped the shrimp in the sink. "That's okay," he told Mike. "Bramwell is a character."

It seemed the whole world was upside down this day. Now Sherman Grove was trying to put Mike Harbinger at ease.

"Listen," Mike assured Sherman, "relatives can be harder to figure out than strangers. You're good at it."

Sherman was overcome with confusion. Not only was somebody offering him respect, the somebody was Mike Harbinger. "Well, I . . . I think about people a lot."

"He reads everything," I put in hastily, trying to redeem myself. *"Born to Win; I'm O.K., You're O.K.; When I Say No, I Feel Guilty*—he's got them all upstairs."

"I've never read much psychology." Mike put Jake down. "I like books about science, though."

Jake scurried back and forth, sniffing the floor.

"Did you ever read *The Medusa and the Snail*?" Sherman asked Mike. "Or *The Crack in the Cosmic Egg* or *The Dragons of Eden*?"

"I've never even heard of them," Mike confessed.

"I could loan them to you," Sherman offered hesitantly.

"Great!" Mike said. "Should we feed the dog before he gets any more frustrated?"

Sherman took a can off the counter and headed for the back door with Mike. Jake followed.

"Do you have a computer?" Sherman asked Mike. The door closed behind them.

Left alone in the kitchen, I washed my hands. I let the cold water run as I shoved the shrimp and shells into the drain, then turned on the garbage disposal. To my relief, the shrimp and the water went down.

I knew that if we didn't get some food into the dining room, Mrs. Grove would soon be even more frantic. I transferred the rest of the bowls and trays and platters from the cooking island to the serving

117

cart, and wheeled it over to the counter at the left of the sink. Shrimp were scattered among the bread slices and cracker boxes.

The counter to the right of the sink was a jumble of tubs and jars and cans and bottles, stray shrimp, and the bags of chips and boxes of cereal that Sherman had knocked off the shelf.

It seemed wise to work with what I could identify. Clearing a space on the counter in front of me, I pulled the cart over and selected a few bowls and trays. Then I spooned what I was almost certain was guacamole dip from a tub into a bowl and put the bowl on a tray. After I arranged corn chips around the bowl, I began to feel encouraged. I filled another bowl with what looked as if it might be clam dip and surrounded it with potato chips.

Mike and Sherman came in from the garage, both talking at once. I arranged some barbecue chips around what was very likely a blue cheese dip.

"Hey, neat!" Sherman passed one tray to Mike and took another.

Holding the trays high like waiters, they carried my handiwork into the dining room.

Guests seemed to be arriving in droves. I could hear talking, even laughing, getting louder and louder. Though I was feeling a lot of pressure to get more food out there, I began to get caught up in the challenge. I brought bread and crackers over to the right-hand counter, and started spreading them with whatever was opened and seemed like the

118

right consistency. Some of the stuff in the cans smelled pretty rank, but what did I know about gourmet food?

Mike and Sherman returned. "We're just putting everything on the dining room table," Sherman said.

"That's okay with me." I went on working.

Sherman began gathering up shrimp from the counter.

"There must be a hundred people out there," Mike told me, as if he talked to girls with stubble cuts every day.

"Pat Troup's here, too." Sherman put the shrimp on a platter.

When the people with you act as if you look fine, you begin to forget that you don't. "You mean as a reporter?" I asked.

"Naturally. My parents would only invite *editors* socially."

Mike shook pickled onions out of an open jar onto the platter.

"Wait a minute," I said to Sherman. "This party is for your dad to tell all these important people that he's running for mayor, before he announces it publicly."

Sherman emptied a jar of mixed nuts around the shrimp and onions. "There's no point inviting important people if it's not in the paper that they were here. It's an evening paper, Dez, and this is Sunday. The story of the party and the story of his announcement at the press conference will be in the same edition tomorrow."

Mike opened a box of little crackers and handed it to me. "It's very important to important people that everybody knows the candidate told them he was running before he told anybody else."

"Right." Sherman circled the nuts with a ring of marinated mushrooms. "There's more to politics, Dez, than anybody who's not in it suspects."

I kept on spreading one thing after another on bread and crackers. Mike and Sherman carried trays and platters into the dining room.

We were looking around for more serving dishes when Mrs. Grove came charging into the kitchen, carrying one of the platters I'd filled. "This will not do at all! At all!" She slammed the tray down before me on the center island. "You must garnish the canapés. And *who* is dumping cocktail onions and marinated mushrooms and nuts on the same tray? This is not a scout jamboree!"

She stormed back into the dining room.

Ordinarily, Sherman would have been upset by his mother's display, but being accepted by Mike Harbinger had made him a little reckless. "Garnish. Garnish." He ambled over to the counter and held up an unopened jar of pimientos. "This has got to be garnish. Nobody would eat it plain."

"We'd better get rid of some of this junk so we'll know the garnish from the garbage," Mike said.

"There are paper bags under the sink," Sherman told him.

Mike took a bag from under the sink, opened it, and put it on the floor. He began tossing empty containers from my counter into it.

Shirley came in from the dining room and went to the refrigerator. "Bring me a bowl, somebody. We need more ice for the bar."

I went on with my work. Sherman took her a bowl.

Bramwell stuck his head in. "Somebody has to drive Councilman Barrows to a service station," he told Shirley. "You want to come along?"

She handed the bowl to Sherman and left with Bramwell.

"She does seem to be getting flighty," Sherman told me.

Mike scooped up more empty cans from the counter.

"Hey!" Sherman grabbed his arm. "What did that label say?"

Mike put the cans down on the counter again. "Which one?"

"That one." Sherman's voice dwindled.

Mike picked up the can Sherman was staring at. "It's just dog food . . ."

Sherman dashed toward the laundry room, Mike and me behind him.

seven

Jake's dish was on the floor. Sherman reached into the wastebasket beside the dryer and drew out a lint-covered can, which he held as if it were a scorpion. He blew the lint off the can, but then his courage failed him, and he handed the can to Mike, who looked at it soberly.

"Um ... your dog just ate a fortune in truffles," Mike told him gently.

Sherman groaned. "Just changing dog food *brands* upsets his stomach."

"Wait. Wait." Dreadful as it was, someone had to say it. "If you fed Jake the can of truffles, and the dog food can in the kitchen is empty—"

We raced back through the kitchen, Jake with us. As Mike shoved open the swinging door, Jake shot past him into the dining room.

There must have been more than a hundred people standing with their backs to us. Before us was the long dining room table, with a huge ice sculpture in the shape of our City Hall and flowers and

122

linens and silver and china—and plates and plates of the canapés I'd made so efficiently, the canapés Sherman and Mike had carried so cheerfully through the swinging doors.

The guests were gathered at the other end of the dining room, where it joined the living room.

Most of them were holding drinks and little plates of food. Everyone was quiet as Harley Grove spoke. Even the dog was silent as he strolled into the crowd.

"Sherman," I whispered, "I can't tell which canapés have what on them."

Mike reached for a platter. "Let's get them all off the table."

"But what about the ones the people already took?" I tried to keep my voice steady.

I couldn't see Harley Grove over the crowd, but he certainly didn't sound like a man who'd been struggling with fires and plumbing. Of course, he didn't know about the refreshments yet.

His voice was deep and rich and sincere. "And I promise you all an administration dedicated to reform, to progress, to prosperity . . ."

I heard Sherman take a quick deep breath before he yelled, "DON'T ANYBODY SWALLOW ANYTHING!"

The crowd parted as Mrs. Grove advanced upon us like a storm trooper. She shoved Sherman through the swinging door so fast that Mike and I had to back into the kitchen or be flattened by him.

"How dare you!" Mrs. Grove gave Sherman another shove.

123

A silver-haired man charged in from the dining room. Behind him came Mrs. Harbinger and then Pat Troup, carrying Jake.

"Sherman tried to help!" Mike Harbinger told Mrs. Grove.

The silver-haired man grabbed Mike's arm. "You keep out of this!"

"Dad, will you just be calm?" Mike sounded aggrieved but patient.

"You take your hands off him!" Mike's mother flared at his father.

"Hey! Hey! Hey!" Bramwell came through the swinging door, Shirley behind him. "What are you landing all over the kids for?"

Mrs. Grove suddenly noticed Pat Troup. "Do you mind?" she snapped.

"Whose dog?" Pat asked me. "He doesn't seem to like councilmen."

"Mom," Sherman said desperately, "we've got to get the canapés away from the people out there."

"Don't try to change the subject!"

Looking at me, Mike jerked his head toward the dining room. As I eased toward the door, Mrs. Grove straightened. "Don't you dare set a foot in there, Desdemona Blank!"

Sherman looked ready to cry. "Mom, what they've got in there are dog-food canapés."

His mother's hands slid down his arms. She sank into a squat, her elbows on her knees and her head in her hands. "Don't explain. Don't."

"Dear?" Opening the swinging door, Mr. Grove

124

looked in. His face was drawn, but his voice was bright and hearty. "The last guests are leaving, dear. Won't you come out and say goodbye?"

Bramwell helped Mrs. Grove up. She tried to head for the back door, but he turned her toward the dining room, and the Harbingers followed her through. They must have been good friends of hers, or very staunch supporters of Harley's.

"Dog-food canapés?" Shirley asked Sherman.

"I got the cans mixed up, so I dumped truffles in the dog dish and we spread dog food on the bread and crackers."

We. Even in despair, Sherman was careful to protect me.

"You print a word about this..." Bramwell warned Pat.

"I wouldn't wait until tomorrow's edition to tell your guests they ate dog food," she said.

"Oh, come on," Bramwell scoffed. "Nobody's going to eat canned dog food. Did you ever *smell* the stuff? I wouldn't feed it to my dog."

"Dog? You mean Jake?" Harley Grove reentered the kitchen with his wife and the Harbingers. "The dog who attacked Councilman Barrows? The dog who belongs to my son? My son, who is dedicated to the destruction of my political future, my social life, any position I had in this community, not to mention my mental health."

"Come off it, Harley," Mrs. Harbinger said. "You're going to scar your child for life."

Glancing at Pat Troup, Mrs. Grove patted her

125

husband's arm. "Harley. Harley, it will all look brighter tomorrow."

He glared at Pat. "It will all look much darker tomorrow, in bold black print."

"I'm a reporter, not a gossip columnist," she said coldly.

"I respect that," Bramwell declared. "And the dog food was approved by the Department of Agriculture. Nobody will get sick from eating dog-food canapés. On the other hand, it would probably make them sick to read that they ate them."

"Dog-food canapés?" Harley Grove looked at his brother wildly.

Mrs. Grove put a firm hand on Bramwell's arm. "It's been a long day, and I know you all want to help us clean up, but we can take care of it. We don't want to keep you lovely people. The party is over—all's well that ends well."

"Ends well? More than a hundred guests inhaling soot. Guests who approach the bathroom and are harassed by two women in pink uniforms and great monuments of technologically advanced hair . . ." Harley Grove drew a deep breath as Mona and Lisa strolled in from the hall.

Mrs. Grove never stopped smiling, but she kept her grip on her husband's arm.

He seemed to have a need to talk. "We spend a fortune for a caterer, and the food comes out looking like party snacks for a fraternity hazing. When I finally announce my candidacy, my son, my own

126

flesh and blood, bursts in, bellowing, *'Don't swallow anything!'* " Mr. Grove pried his wife's fingers off his arm. "I had every reason to expect this day to end in congratulations, pledges, donations. Instead, more than one hundred people skulked out of here like the survivors of a weekend at the Draculas'.... Dog-food canapés?"

"Later, dear," Mrs. Grove told him.

Everyone else was silent. Everyone seemed drained.

Everyone but Mona and Lisa. They leaned against the refrigerator, looking more relaxed than I'd ever seen them.

Mrs. Harbinger took the caterer's apron off the food processor. "There's nothing to do about it now, except clean up."

She was right. I'd come there with fantasies of winning over Sherman's parents and uncle. Instead, I had helped create a calamity they'd never forget. I suspected that if Pat Troup hadn't been there, they'd have ordered me out long ago.

"I'll just take out some of the trash." Bramwell picked up a bag. "Then we've got to get going. My dog will be thinking I'm never coming back."

"You want a ride?" Pat asked me.

I hesitated. "My father ..." I glanced at Shirley, but she was busy throwing canapés into the sink.

"Why don't you call him?" Pat suggested. "Tell him I'll run you home."

After tormenting you mercilessly, fate tosses you

127

a token favor. At least I didn't have to worry about arranging my departure so that my father wouldn't run into Shirley.

He was home, of course, and happy to hear that he didn't have to come out again.

I got my coat and tied on Mrs. Farisee's scarf, although it didn't matter anymore.

Pat was in the foyer wearing a plum-color tweed cape and her loose-knit green-and-tan-and-purple Dr. Who muffler. She glanced into the parlor, where Mona and Lisa were collecting empty glasses. "Anybody need a ride?"

"Thanks anyway," Mona said. "We told Mr. Wonderful we'd stick around until he's ready to leave."

"Besides," Lisa added, "we want to see how it turns out."

Mona watched Pat toss the muffler around her head and shoulders. "Who does your hair?" she asked.

"In the annals of weird," Pat observed, as her car wheezed and sputtered into life, "that party will live forever. You're not going to cry, are you?"

"Not if I can help it." The next thing I knew, I was telling her about my polyurethaned hair and the Groves' condominium plans.

"I thought that if I helped them in an emergency, they might be so grateful they'd at least find us another place to live if they did sell our house. And you saw what happened."

"Condos," Pat said. "They're a plague. Instead of fixing up perfectly livable little houses, the owners sell them to developers who tear them down and put up fancy buildings the people they evicted can't afford to live in. There was a rash of them years ago, and the builders lost their shirts. But the craze is starting again. I'm going to write a series on it."

"Will that do any good?"

"Probably not. The City Council is all for redevelopment and the big moneylenders have a stake in it."

"You're going to write about it anyway?"

"That's my job. I guess a reporter always thinks that if she can explain what's going on, it may make a difference. That's supposed to compensate for our lousy wages."

She drove on for another block. I was quiet, thinking how I was obsessed with my haircut, which was nothing compared to a family and three dogs without a home.

"This deal," Pat said, "has some interesting ingredients. We've got Harley, running for mayor, pushing through the condo conversions, and presently owning the houses that will be razed for them. We've got his brother, who you say will be buying the houses. Then we've got my dad, refusing to make it easy for them. When he hears that they're planning to destroy his house for a condo. . . ." She grinned. "He wouldn't sell now for anything."

I couldn't see what she was so optimistic about. "Can't they make him? Sherman said that since

129

Bramwell will own most of the houses on the block, it should be a cinch to get your father's condemned."

"Ah ha! But now we come to the crucial ingredients, the wild cards. We've got Desdemona Blank, and Pat Troup, ace reporter. They were at the party at which over one hundred backers of Harley Grove's mayoral campaign were served dog food. Both you and I know we would never lower ourselves to hold that over the Groves. But *they* don't. Neither your father nor mine is in any danger of being forced to find another dwelling for a long, long time."

I just rode along for a while, letting it sink in that we might actually be safe. Within a few blocks, I could even think about other people's problems. "I hope Sherman's parents won't be too rough on him."

"He's kind of a wispy kid."

"Most people think he's a wimp." Then I told her what my father had said about wimps.

Her face grew stern and her voice was firm. "No. Not Bruce Springsteen. Never. Bruce Springsteen is reason to believe."

I hoped she wasn't going to start talking religion, but I had to ask. "In what?"

"The species."

When we stopped at my house, she said, "Listen, your hair will grow. Look at me. I won't."

"Lots of guys like short girls."

"Big deal. You know how far that gets you in my line of work? Half my life, I've been fighting *cute*."

When I came in, my father turned off "60 Minutes." He was still in his suit trousers and shirt, and he hadn't even taken off his shoes. I suppose he wanted to be ready to hurry out if Shirley called.

I could hear the television in the bedroom and the radio in Mrs. Farisee's room.

I couldn't help thinking of the Groves, three people in a house so big they couldn't even hear one another most of the time: three people with three and a half bathrooms.

On the other hand, ours was working.

"How was it?" My father tossed the TV listing on an end table, to make room for me beside him on the sofa.

I took off my coat and the scarf and sat down. "You don't want to know."

I told him anyway, the whole dreadful business.

". . . So I wrecked the party by making dog-food canapés—which are probably all that will keep him from kicking us out of this house. Pat says they'll think we might use the canapés against them."

"Sure they will, because they'd use it if the positions were reversed. So you saved your family and our dogs—not to mention Mr. Troup."

"Mr. Troup wouldn't thank me if I saved this whole town."

Putting an arm around me, my father pulled me closer. "He might find it hard to say 'Thank you,

Desdemona, for serving dog food to your landlord's guests.' That's true. But remember that your intentions were noble, and the outcome will be fine."

That did it. "You know, if anybody had tried to tell me an hour ago that I would ever smile again, I would have been insulted."

He cuddled my head against his shoulder and ran a hand over my hair. "Feels like a Chesapeake Bay retriever." Then he got serious. "Harley can't lose this election, Dez. He's got the paper and most of the City Council behind him—even Councilman Barrows, public rest room or no." He was quiet for a minute, and I could tell he wasn't thinking of me or of elections. "You say Shirley was there with Harley's brother?"

I sat up so I could look at him. "I wasn't sure I should tell you, but I decided it would be better if I did. You won't have to try to look unsurprised if you hear about it from somebody else."

He nodded. "You were right."

"I thought you and she were getting along."

"So did I."

"You feel bad?"

"Yes."

I noticed that he'd been biting his cuticles again. He probably did it rather than smoke, which might leave his children prematurely fatherless. He was a good man, kind to children and dogs, and I couldn't understand why things seemed to go right for him so seldom. "There's got to be something wrong with her."

"Of course," he said gravely. "Who's going to take a rich, handsome bachelor with a thirty-thousand-dollar car over a married father of three who's renting a two-bedroom house from . . ."

I pulled away. "That really bothers me, when you make jokes to cover up how you feel. I'm serious. What does she see in him?"

"Aside from . . ."

"No, come on. Don't. He's . . ."

"Crass? Abrasive?"

"At his best. And all you know about him is what I've told you, remember?"

"What about the dog? What about him defending you and Sherman at the party?"

"Mrs. Harbinger defended Mike and Sherman, but that doesn't make her Mother of the Year. You're not going to tell me Bramwell has a heart of gold."

"I'm saying there's probably a lot more to him than you see. Look how different from Harley he is. Did they grow up as privileged as you'd guess from meeting Harley, or on the mean streets you'd expect from what you saw of Bramwell? Maybe what fascinates Shirley is that he is so complex."

My father was actually getting absorbed in his analysis. The man had just been *dumped,* and he was getting into character studies. For a second, I could see how he could drive a woman dating him right to somebody who reacted more and talked less. Immediately, I felt disloyal. "But Shirley's so different from Sherman's uncle," I protested.

133

"She's not engaged to him, Dez. Besides, do you think I'm attracted only to women with high I.Q.'s and higher principles?"

I did not smile. I laughed, just thinking of the women he had dated after my mother left and before he met Shirley. "They run together in my mind—a lot of lip gloss and satin blouses and barely voting age."

The telephone rang and he went to answer it.

He came back looking bemused. "Pat Troup. She wants to know if I'd like to go out for pizza."

I was amazed. "You going?"

"Sure."

"Oh, good." Pat was loaded with I.Q. and principles. Also, she was a woman of action, which is what a man who tends not to be needs.

After my father left, I went back to the bedroom. Preston and my brother were playing Chinese checkers on the floor while Preston talked, and talked. Neither of them greeted me.

When I left the room, Aida followed.

"Can't you tell them you want to play, too?" I asked her.

She shook her head and followed me to the parlor and didn't even object to the television program I selected.

After a while, a car's horn sounded.

A minute later, I heard someone knock on Mrs. Farisee's door, and then Preston's voice. "Good night, Mrs. Farisee. Thank you for the very nice time."

She walked him to the door, and helped him turn up the collar of his navy blue double-breasted wool coat.

"What a charmer," she said when he left. She looked at me. "How was the party?"

I turned down the set. "I think I'm getting the flu."

"You're going to school tomorrow. Your hair won't be that much longer Tuesday."

eight

I did feel sick when I woke and remembered my hair.

I knew it would do no good to appeal to my father. He'd tell me the same thing Mrs. Farisee had.

With five people and one bathroom, mornings are difficult, so we never chat at breakfast the way families are supposed to.

Aida seemed to have no more appetite than I, but both my father and Antony ate their waffles with zest.

When the telephone rang, Mrs. Farisee answered it, and then told the caller, "After this, don't phone at breakfast time."

That gave me no clue who it was. Mrs. Farisee wouldn't hesitate to instruct the President not to call us at breakfast time.

"For you," she told Antony.

"May I be excused?" Aida asked, when he went to the telephone.

"Isn't anybody going to eat this morning?" my father demanded.

Aida left the table.

My brother came back. "Can I go to Preston's after school?" he asked my father.

"*May* I go, and did his mother invite you?"

Antony nodded. "She'll drive me home."

"Fine. But hurry up and finish your breakfast." My father poured himself another cup of coffee.

Sherman arrived to walk to school with Antony and me.

Walking to school with Mrs. Farisee's paisley print scarf on, I was grateful for the company of even my brother and an eleven-year-old kid.

"How's Jake?" I asked Sherman.

"Fine. Kind of put out that he didn't get truffles for breakfast."

"What happened after I left?"

"My father stewed and my mother went to bed with a migraine right after the Harbingers left."

Neither of us mentioned Bramwell buying our house. Sherman probably didn't want to remind me of how seriously I'd offended his parents. I certainly wasn't going to bring up the reason we'd probably be staying. You don't tell your best friend that his parents would think you capable of blackmail.

Ahead of us, I saw some people walking to school. Suddenly, a roof over my head meant nothing compared to the stubble on my head. "Sherman, I'm going to be sick. I'm going to be sick right here on the sidewalk. This scarf is bad enough, but I can never, never show my hair to a whole school."

He stopped. "You don't want anybody to notice you, so you're going to throw up. You want humiliation, try throwing up in public. I did, my first day in kindergarten. Right in the classroom."

He walked on, and I fell into step, rather than be left with only a five-year-old.

"I'm talking instant celebrity," Sherman continued somberly. "Everybody yells and jumps away and makes a big production of pretending to gag. Then the custodian comes along with a ton of sawdust and cleans up, and all day everybody goes 'Yuck' when you come near."

My brother walked between us, gazing up at Sherman with awe.

I was impressed, in spite of myself. "How about if I just pass out?"

He didn't even look at me. "Great way to be inconspicuous. With any luck, somebody will call an ambulance, and they'll roar up with that old red light flashing and load you on a stretcher and rush you to the emergency room and call your father at work..."

"Sherman, I am truly, physically sick." I was not exaggerating. My heart seemed to be moving up in my chest, crowding my lungs, squeezing all the breath out of me.

We had reached the corner of the street Mike Harbinger usually came down. Since I didn't dare turn back and go home, the only thing to do now was hurry on. I walked faster, looking straight ahead.

"Hey, Sherman!"

I knew the voice.

Mike Harbinger was hailing Sherman Grove.

I was so astonished, I looked before I thought.

"Hey, Antony!" Preston broke away from the group trailing his brother and ran toward us.

Sherman stopped. Antony stopped.

When Mike Harbinger yelled, everybody looked. It was too late to run.

Preston started talking even before he reached us. Behind him came a gaggle of boys about my brother's size. Closing rapidly were Mike and his friends.

I don't know whether my legs simply failed me, or whether my reactions to the stresses of the last few days reached a critical point. Suddenly I was sitting on somebody's front lawn.

"Hey." Dropping his books beside me, Mike hunkered down to peer in my face. "Are you all right, Dez?"

I should have thrown up when I had the chance, I thought. *I should have fainted.* A person like me could do almost anything without attracting the notice she'd get just by being with Mike Harbinger.

"You look pale." His face was only inches from mine. "You want me to walk you home?"

"She's all right," Sherman said. "She just doesn't want to show her hair."

I could sink my teeth into his ankle, I thought,

139

but he probably has his tetanus boosters up to date.

"What's the matter with your hair?" Mike asked me.

"You ought to see it," Preston told the little kids around him. "Like she ran her head through a lawn mower."

Mike sat down beside me. "We'll wait for a few minutes. Then if you don't feel better I'll phone somebody to come get you. Preston, you guys go on."

"Go ahead," I told my brother.

As Antony walked away with Preston and Preston's group, Mike yelled after them, "Hey! You two come directly home after school, hear?"

Preston nodded and waved and kept talking to Antony.

Mike looked up at Sherman, who stood over us. "I tried the computer program you showed me after the party, but I'm still missing something."

Sherman sat down to explain. Mike's friends sat down to listen. Every few words, one of them would interrupt with a question—for Sherman.

"I still don't get it," Mike said finally.

"Why don't we all go to my house after school and you can show us." A tall dark-haired boy with a tan that made him look like a ski instructor had been frowning over Sherman's explanation. "I've got a hard disk and dual drives," he told Sherman, as if presenting his credentials.

"He's also got an eight-millimeter camcorder and

140

a laser disk player with Dolby hi-fi remote stereo," a redhead added.

"And every video Huey Lewis ever made," the dark-haired boy said modestly.

"You're kidding!" Sherman gasped.

"Right back to 'Do You Believe in Love?' and 'Workin' for a Livin'.' Maybe you can figure out why I'm still getting noise on my tapes."

We sat there, Sherman and I, surrounded by high school superstars talking about their computers and audio and video equipment.

Mike looked at me. "Are you going to be all right?" he asked.

I nodded.

He gathered up my books and even steadied me as I stood. Then he and his friends walked Sherman and me to the junior high school, Mike carrying my books. I would have felt stupid letting him, except that I knew he was doing it because I was feeling shaky, not because I was a female.

As we approached the school's entrance, crowds parted before us.

I realized, suddenly and very clearly, that I could get away with my haircut. I could get away with having Sherman for a friend. I could get away with anything short of double-knit polyester.

Mike Harbinger had walked to school with me.

"I'm okay now." I took my books. "Thanks."

"Meet you here at three-thirty," he told Sherman.

"You can call home from my house," said the boy

141

with the Dolby hi-fi remote stereo video disk player.

Sherman watched them walk on toward the high school. "Can you imagine my parents if I went anyplace but your house without calling for permission *first*?"

All around us, people were watching us, so he kept his voice low. "I'm going to have to go to the office and try to con the school secretary into letting me use the phone."

I thought of Sherman calling from school for permission to hang out with a bunch of high school luminaries, and I struggled to keep my face solemn.

"It's not funny." He looked hurt.

I walked in the front door with him. "I'm just picturing all those overprivileged overachievers in their classy watches and sixty-dollar shirts sitting around listening to 'Workin' for a Livin'."

"Hey, twenty years from now those Huey Lewis tapes will still be classics."

"I know! I know! Would Mike Harbinger's associates be guilty of having less-than-impeccable taste? And twenty years from now . . . No. No, they won't be selling cars or working in little offices. They'll own their family's dealerships and law firms, but they'll still be telling everybody how they used to watch those old music videos with you."

"You're crazy this morning, you know that?"

"Sure I'm crazy. Suddenly, I don't see you as eleven. You're almost twelve. Mike Harbinger talks to you."

"You don't have to be so sarcastic about him. He likes you."

I grabbed Sherman's sleeve, right there in the crowded hall. "How do you know?"

"After you left yesterday, he said you were neat. He asked how old you were."

It was too much. I let my hand drop.

"I told him thirteen."

"Sherman." Naturally, I couldn't embarrass my best friend by saying *I love you.*

"He also likes your hair," Sherman added.

I dodged in front of him. *"What? What?"*

"He says it reminds him of Annie."

"Annie?"

"Annie Lennox. You know, the Eurythmics singer."

"You let me suffer all morning and you didn't tell me?"

"I forgot."

I would have chased him to his locker, but I wasn't so secure that I would deliberately make a scene while wearing a paisley print scarf on my head.

As I turned down the corridor to my own locker, two girls fell into step with me.

"How long have you known him?" Marti Dunnigan was our class president. Her best friend, Kerri White, had nominated her, and then Marti nominated Kerri for vice-president, and they both won.

"Sherman?" I asked.

"Him." Kerri's voice was urgent. "You know."

"Oh, Mike. We went to the van Gogh exhibit Saturday night, and we were at a party yesterday."

Marti smote her own forehead with the heel of her hand. "Art? He likes *art*? And I went *skating* Saturday!"

Kerri, who had never worn the same sweater twice in a month, picked a piece of lint off my sleeve.

I hung my coat in my locker and fussed around with my books.

"You forgot to take your scarf off," Kerri reminded me.

I didn't feel like the girl Mike had walked to school with, suddenly.

I could make a dash for the rest room, but I couldn't cower in there all day. I could say I was sick, but Mrs. Farisee wouldn't let me stay home. If I went anywhere else, the school would call my house, and then I'd be in trouble that would make my hours at the Groves' party seem pleasant.

There was no way out. Someday, I knew, I would look back on this moment, and it would still seem excruciating.

I took off the scarf.

Marti struck her forehead again. "How did you make your folks *let* you?"

I was still the girl who had walked to school with Mike Harbinger. Everything about me was right. Especially my hair, because nobody in the school had a cut like mine, and Mike Harbinger had walked to school with me.

144

"My mother would kill me if I even showed her a picture of a cut like that!" Kerri stared at me. "I had to beg for months just to get tinted contact lenses! How did you talk your folks into it?"

"I didn't."

She was staggered. "You mean you just went down and got it cut?"

It's hard work to maintain a pose. "Actually," I confessed, "it got Varathaned, and—"

"You mean like *varnished*?" Marti cried, with such feeling that a couple of other girls hurried over to us.

"She varnished her hair!" Kerri announced.

Teena Brannigan edged past Kerri to touch my hair. "It *is*! It's stiff!"

"Let me see." Laurelle Carson patted my head.

Marti stepped back to squint at me. "You know what would be fan*tas*tic? If you colored it, maybe platinum, or red."

Kerri cast her a look of cold disdain. "That would look like she was *trying*."

"Does Mike like it?" Teena asked.

I wondered if there was anybody in the school building who hadn't seen me with him, or heard about it already.

"Of course he likes it," Kerri said. "He walked to school with her, didn't he?"

"So who did you get to cut it for you without your parents' permission?" Kerri pressed.

"The Mona Lisa," I said, "but only because it was a special case."

145

I started for my homeroom. To be one of the last few sauntering in would be just like challenging my teacher. Laurelle, Teena, Marti, and Kerri fell into step with me, along with three girls who usually cut ahead of me whenever I bought my lunch.

Marti walked backward so she could face me. "The Mona Lisa?"

"In the Rancho Grande Mall," I said.

"That old place? I never knew they could do hair like that!"

Teena looked at her scornfully. "You think *I. Magnin* is going to cut hair like that?" She edged around Laurelle to walk next to me. "Would I have to take in a note from my mother?"

"Absolutely," I assured her. "Or take your mother."

Jerking her head toward me, Kerri told the line-crashers, "She went out with Mike Harbinger last Saturday and Sunday both."

"It wasn't like a date or anything." I think I was reassuring myself, more than anything else. "My father would never let me go out on a real date yet."

Cheryl reclaimed her position next to me. "My mother says I can't go out with boys until I'm *fifteen*."

I slowed down. "You know, there's a lot of stress involved in going anywhere with a guy, even when it's not a real date."

They were all quiet, walking slower, everybody with her own thoughts.

"Yeah," Kerri said finally. "You don't think

about that aspect—until you start thinking about it."

"So you're just kind of friends with Mike?" Marti asked.

I nodded. "We've been through a lot together."

"Imagine." Teena was solemn. "Mike Harbinger for your *friend.*"

"But you like him, don't you?" one of the line-crashers prompted.

I stopped. "I do. I really do." I didn't truly realize it until I said it. "He's a nice guy."

Laurelle fell backward into Kerri's arms. *"A nice guy,"* she moaned.

At roll call, my homeroom teacher glanced at my hair and closed his eyes.

When I walked into my math class, the teacher told me I was wanted in the office. As I walked out, even boys threw me sympathetic grimaces and thumbs-up signs.

"Don't sit down," the school secretary greeted me. "Go right into the office before you attract more fans."

Ms. Cohen, our principal, looked at me across her desk. "I heard, but I still wasn't prepared. The rumor is that it's varnished, too."

I nodded.

Before I could speak, she went on. "I deplore mindless conformity. I respect individuality. It is nobody's business how you wear your hair, so long as it does not constitute a public health hazard. I'm just asking you, one human being to another,

147

whether this is the first shot in a campaign of organized rebellion."

I explained how I came to be Varathaned and shorn.

"I have to admit I'm relieved," she said when I'd finished.

"It could catch on," I warned.

"I can live with it. When I started college, and all the sorority types wore skirts and sweaters, my friends and I walked around barefoot carrying acoustic guitars and wearing bedspreads."

"Bedspreads?"

"Indian, from Cost Plus or Pier One. You fold it over, cut a hole for the head, sew up the sides from about the knees to the armpits..." She stopped suddenly. "Go back to class."

As I started for the door, she said, "I remember, when I was fifteen, my mother asked me why my generation had this irresistible urge to rile hers."

"What did you tell her?"

"I said, 'Because you're there.'"

"I don't want to rile anybody."

"You haven't hit your teens."

Being called to the office only magnified my renown. Everybody wanted to know what Ms. Cohen had said. I didn't mention the bare feet and bedspreads. She'd trusted me.

There's a proverb or something that says, "Be careful what you wish for. You might get it."

At lunch, so many people dragged chairs over to my table, I had to eat with my elbows wedged

148

against my sides. I couldn't even see where Sherman was.

I had notes passed to me in all my classes.

So many people stopped me to talk after school that it was quarter to four by the time I got out of the building.

That part was okay. I wouldn't have wanted to be around when Mike and his friends came for Sherman. With all the twelve- and thirteen-year-old girls trailing me, there would have been just too much going on.

Of course, I doubted that fifteen-year-old males talking electronics would notice any junior high school girls.

What surprised me was that I missed Sherman.

I worried about him a little, too. There's a big gap between fifteen and even a brilliant twelve. By the time Mike and his friends got their driver's licenses, they'd be moving into a world where he'd be lost even as a mascot.

Marti and Kerri ran with me to my sister's school.

Aida was waiting on the sidewalk with a small, dark-haired girl and a slender, anxious-looking woman of about thirty.

Aida, who had scuffed out the right knee of her new jeans and spilled something down the front of her coat, started talking when I was yards away. "Here's my sister." She clutched the hand of the little girl, who smiled at me as if I were a friend from way back.

"This is Tran," Aida told me as I came closer. "She's in my class, and this is her mom. Before I left for school, I asked Mrs. Farisee if I could bring a friend home. It's okay with her, but I don't think it is with Mrs. Luan."

Mrs. Luan smiled at me, but she looked uncertain and embarrassed. She was not much taller than I. Like Tran, she had thick, lustrous, straight black hair and gorgeous almond-shaped eyes. Mrs. Luan wore a thin tan coat with cotton slacks and canvas sneakers. It was clear that what clothing money there was went to dress Tran.

Aida was hanging on to Tran's hand and looking at me as if I could fix everything.

I wasn't sure I could make myself understood, but it was cold and they must have been standing there waiting for me a long time. "See you guys later," I told Marti and Kerri.

They left, and I turned my attention to Mrs. Luan. "We are happy to have Tran come visit. We can even bring her home later, if you like."

Mrs. Luan listened politely, but she still seemed undecided.

I wasn't sure whether she had understood me, but I understood her look. It would be terrifying to just turn your kid loose in a strange country.

"Would you come, too?" I asked her. "Come to tea, please. Mrs. Farisee would want me to invite you." I wasn't sure about that last part, but we couldn't stand in the street negotiating forever.

"Today?" Mrs. Luan asked.

"Yes," I said. "Yes. Now."

"Oh." She smiled again, and she suddenly looked much younger. "Thank you. Yes. Thank you."

Aida and Tran bounded ahead and around and behind us like grasshoppers in spring.

Mrs. Luan's English was new and careful, but, block by block, she became more comfortable trying it out. By the time we got to my house, she'd told me that Tran was her only child, that they had been in this country six months, and that she found it very big and very cold.

You don't often bring a kid home from school with her mother, but Mrs. Farisee didn't betray her surprise. Since I had invited Mrs. Luan, I offered to make her tea. "Fine," Mrs. Farisee said. "I made chocolate chip cookies. They're on top of the fridge."

I was astonished. Aida's bringing home a friend must have been a great occasion in Mrs. Farisee's eyes, too.

I took Mrs. Luan's coat and left her in the parlor with Mrs. Farisee. I could hear them talking while I put on the kettle and set a tea tray.

Aida took Tran directly out to the backyard to meet Herb and Joe and Sadie. Hearing the riotous greetings, I hoped Mrs. Luan would think it was some other dogs in the neighborhood.

Fortunately, we had three good china cups without chipped rims.

Being well-adjusted dogs, ours settled down after the first thrill of meeting a new person. I could hear

Aida showing Tran around. "So this pile of rocks and wood will be our castle, and we and the dogs are the French soldiers in it. Monty Python and Sir Lance-a-Lot are attacking us, and we throw down horrible stuff and yell insults like—"

I ran to the back door. "Aida Blank!" I shouted.

When I carried the tray into the parlor, Mrs. Luan and Mrs. Farisee were chatting almost like neighbors.

After a cup of tea, I excused myself and called Aida and Tran in for cookies. Then I took some back to the bedroom.

It wasn't often I had our room to myself. I lay on my bed, reveling in the solitude. It wasn't much of a room, but at the moment it was all mine.

Of course, if anything developed between Pat Troup and my father, their combined salaries might qualify them for a mortgage.

Four bedrooms would be ideal, but we could scrape by with three, so long as we had two bathrooms.

I wondered how Pat would get along with Mrs. Farisee. She'd have to. We couldn't lose Mrs. Farisee.

One pizza, and I was casting Pat Troup as a potential stepmother. Ridiculous, maybe, but a healthy sign—as much as you may want somebody who's left you, you can't sit around waiting forever.

I felt more guilty about taking Mrs. Farisee for granted. Then I wondered about my assumption that any woman would rather be a reporter than a housekeeper. It might well be that Mrs. Farisee was doing the work she preferred. I wondered what she had wanted, or expected, or hoped for when she was young. I'd never ask her, of course, but it would be interesting if she took a notion to talk about it sometime.

We're separate countries, all of us, separate and mysterious, haunted by the times and places and people we've lost, or never had.

I could hear the women talking in the parlor, and Tran laughing with my sister outside.

There is reason to believe in the species, if you take us one by one.

I brought the dogs into my room. After dinner, I'd call old Sherman and see how he was doing.

ABOUT THE AUTHOR

"I'm in the world of the book when I'm writing," says Beverly Keller. During these times, she doesn't go to the store or clean house, and she lives on crackers and peanut butter. However, her six dogs continue to enjoy a majestic lifestyle, with regular meals and care. In this apparently haphazard fashion, Beverly Keller has created many laugh-aloud books including *No Beasts! No Children!,* which is also about Desdemona and her family.